The Spaniard

By Richard J. Green

1

Los Angeles, West Coast America, 1971

The Pan Am 707 touched down gently onto the hot black runway at LAX a little over half a day after leaving the dark streets of London. Roomy seats, six course meals and free drinks - air travel had certainly changed a great deal since the end of the war.

As the aircraft gently coasted to a halt outside the strange futuristic terminal, he rose from his seat, smoothing out the creases from the thin white trousers of his suit. He slicked back his ebony black hair and took out his photo chromic lens sunglasses; this was LA, not London - his eyes needed time to adjust. The air steward made their standard landing statement over the Tannoy,

"Welcome to Los Angeles Airport. Thank you for flying Pan Am. We hope to see you again soon."

The fake American air hostesses smiled their fake American smiles as he departed the aircraft, wishing him a 'company' goodbye. Still they were friendly and not unpleasant visually; he thoroughly approved of the current vogue for rising female hemlines.

The golden Californian sunset kissed the horizon as he walked down the air stairs. The warm polluted wind buoyed him gently, welcoming him to this very new city on the edge of the Western world. It was warm like the Middle East, not unlike his motherland but not as humid as Indochina and so very, very new. There wasn't much history here but still an awful lot of politics and where people gather in large groups history is bound to be made.

2

Walking towards the terminal, sun glinted through the fronds of distant palm trees lining the main strip outside the airport. A weird flying saucer of a building dominated the skyline. It was a steel and glass 1950's vision of the future. Yep, one day we'll all live on the moon and eat pills for dinner. Well so far - apart from two great nations throwing men in tin cans into the inky blackness of space - we're still waiting for that one to come to fruition.

And it was this business between these two great giants that had brought him to Los Angeles. Less these days of all-out war in some third world backwater; like two children fighting over a favourite toy. No, today's Great Game was more likely to be found in smaller skirmishes on the peripheries of civilised society.

Pausing, he slipped on his jacket, thin white cotton with a very pale thin Oxford blue pinstripe almost unperceivable. Bespoke, it was made in the style of the day at the more fashionable and, more importantly, cheaper Soho end of Saville Row. He had a small leather suitcase with him; carry-on luggage only, he'd be here briefly. Just long enough to check for wind, dial in the range, exhale and hold, then gently squeeze, not pull, the trigger … and breathe.

3

Lodestar Operations, Whitehall, London

… 24 hours earlier

He waited in the reception area for his meeting. It was a beautiful three-storey Georgian building constructed of Portland limestone, but its days as an imperious residency for some grand Regency family were long gone. A NATO green coloured carpet, curling at the corners, covered most of the floor and drab, utilitarian office furniture was spread around the room; chairs, filing cabinets and a grim modern ersatz wood reception desk. There was a standard lamp that looked like it had been pilfered from a disused army barracks, as did the dented grey filing cabinet. The mismatched furniture didn't blend well with the grand marble fireplace, the Georgian stucco and the impossibly tall windows. The only two exceptions to the cheap furnishing were the twin green leather wingback armchairs, in one of which he sat, and a life-sized oil painting of the founder of the company on the wall behind the receptionist.

Knight Commander of the British Empire Ernest Fraser, now Lord no less, wearing full dress uniform in his later years looking imperious and gazing out across some exotic land. Pretty clichéd and he knew the old man hated it, but it was good for business. It reassured the ex-military types and gave the civilians a sense of security. Which are what private military companies are all about.

The intercom buzzed loudly on the receptionist's desk and a cut glass male voice requested,

"Send him in please Caroline."

4

The receptionist was in her late twenties and blonde, but she dressed like a woman her mother's age; long thick skirt and a white blouse buttoned up the neck. Probably an officer's daughter who's almost given up trying to trap a commissioned husband. She briefly glanced towards him and continued bashing the ancient black typewriter.

"He'll see you now."

He stood up, glancing towards the oil painting and wishing it was this man he'd be meeting. A hero of the Desert war in '42, a legend in the Italian campaign and one of the reasons that most of SE Asia was still part of the free world. The man he was meeting was another matter.

Past the large double doors, he entered a large opulent room - again with the odd touch of faded glory; the marble fireplace had a battered three-bar electric heater in front of it. A thin man, in a bespoke suit with swept back blonde hair rose from behind a mahogany desk.

"Ah there you are, please, come in and sit down."

Barely out of his twenties Thomas Fraser was the old man's son. He was a former major with the Signals Corps and he'd served in Cyprus, Ireland and Aden but mostly from behind the frontline. Despite this, he was now the man in charge of Lodestar Operations, following a stroke that'd seen Sir Ernest pensioned off to a quiet life in an Eastbourne nursing home. That probably suited the son; he doubted it suited Sir Ernest.

"Good to see you again. Been quite a while hasn't it."

It was of course a rhetorical question; they hadn’t contacted him for two years. Fraser took a cigarette from a gold box, lit it with an expensive gold lighter and exhaled, looking him up and down.

"Yes ‘69 Oman - trouble with the local tribes if I remember correctly?"

Fraser smiled and he smiled back. It was an emotionless, thousand-yard stare, dead eyes looking right through the man stood in front of him in a handmade suit but with no backbone. You can’t spend the majority of your adult life in the military and special forces without developing a kind of numbness to the trivia of civilian life. Fraser, he assumed, was thinking all about the negotiation they were about to have and how he’d come out on top of the deal. He, meanwhile, was as concerned about this as he was about whether the windows on the building had been cleaned recently or if the elderly security guard at the entrance would wish him farewell, or how much pressure he’d need to exert around Fraser’s neck to get him to pass out. Not much, he thought.

Fraser exhaled expensive cigarette smoke in his direction.

"Would you like a drink old man?"

He pointed a finger in his direction and without waiting for a response.

"Yes of course you would; still Scotch, is it?"

He nodded and looked across the room to a seat in the corner in which sat a blonde giant of a man dressed in a light blue summer suit with loafers - it was February. A friend from across the Atlantic, he mused? With his back towards him, Fraser busied himself at the drinks trolley by the large window overlooking Whitehall. He glanced back towards him.

"Have you been keeping well?"

He took a thin cigar from a leather wallet and lit it, taking the gold Dupont lighter from Fraser's desk. He then unceremoniously tossed the lighter back onto the desk's green leather inlay. It left a mark.

"What do you want, Fraser?"

Fraser, shocked at the directness of the question, almost dropped one of the glasses as he poured the drink. He handed the large man in the summer suit a scotch and soda and neat whisky for the two Englishmen. Fraser smiled and raised his glass towards him as if to say 'Good Health'. He repeated,

"What do you want?"

"Come on old chap no need for you to be so forthright. We're just going to have a little chat here about the old days, the present days and erm the future. More importantly the company and how *you* can help us."

He took a hit from the cigar and exhaled, chasing it with a small nip of the Scotch.

"And why, would I want to do that?"

"Money. Lots and lots of the stuff!"

Both Fraser and the American looked at each other and laughed.

Los Angeles Interstate 405

He had picked the taxi up outside LAX; the driver had hailed him out of his driver's window in heavily accented English as he left the main terminal.

"Hey Mister, Señor, hey taxi cheap taxi."

The cab drove out of the airport and through a series of industrial centres which obviously either catered for, or were owned by, the airlines. Tall bland buildings surrounded by high fences and razor wire, to keep out opportunist thieves, he thought. Unlike most of the airports he'd ever been to, the logistical operations of LAX far exceeded the confines of the airport itself. It wasn't just a cinderblock building in a field with an airstrip surrounded by jungle, desert or wasteland. There were miles of service roads, warehouses, car parks; this was something else.

The car pulled onto a major highway with numerous lanes, and they sped past unfamiliar suburbs, towns and areas. Lennox, Westchester, Inglewood, Fox Hills, West LA, Del Rey, Culver West Mar Vista; they all sounded exotic and unknown; but then no more than a hundred other places he'd fought in. Driving underneath other roads and bridges the air was yellow, thick with smog and the landscape was barren and hot. Now and then you'd glimpse some greenery on a hill but mostly it was unforgiving: mile after mile of flat concrete punctuated by the odd tall building. The sun began to sink further below the horizon. The day had almost given up the good fight and dusk was nearly night.

He wound down the window in the rear of the car and let his hand play with the slip stream as they motored along the five-lane highway - passing or being passed by other traffic. Huge juggernauts lumbered by and they in turn passed muscle cars, compacts and the occasional antique Packard or Studebaker left over from happier times in America. After a while he opened his holdall and took out a small box of Romeo Y Julieta cigars from a beautiful wooden box made of Spanish cedar. He clipped the end with a cutter and lit the smoke. Exhaling Cuban smoke out of the window was probably illegal on this side of the boarder but what the hell, so was what he was here to do.

"First time in LA, Señor?"

The driver was looking in the rear-view mirror of the battered gypsy cab.

"Si, nunca he estado tan lejos al oeste antes."

He told the driver he'd never been this far west before. The driver looked at him in astonishment and replied in his mother tongue

"Mexicano?"

"No, Espanole, I'm Spanish, I come from Asturias."

The driver looked at him through the rearview mirror.

"Ahh yes the green eyes, I can see it in you."

"Are you a native to LA?"

"No Guadalajara. I came here in the 1930s with my parents to work on the farms. Picking fruit, digging ditches anything."

The driver looked tall, for a Mexican, he reckoned around six foot with slate grey hair; white at the sides. He sported a small grey beard and a black shirt. His only homage to extravagance were a pair of yellow tinted driving glasses and a gold tooth when he smiled. He continued,

"And now I have an American passport, I own my own business, and my children go to Gringo college. I am very happy, a Yankee success story."

He smiled wryly. They lapsed into silence as the taxi motored down the highway. Just the occasional double tap of 'duh,duh - duh,duh' as the wheels of the huge car passed over the tamping lines or rumble strips of the interstate. The taxi itself was a huge monster of a Ford, like nothing you'd find in Britain, he imaged it had massive three or four litre engine. It was dark green with a small 'taxi' logo on the side and the leather seats in the rear were ridiculously commodious. You could get six people in the back, back in Guadalajara they probably did.

They began to slow as the car drew up towards another large intersection; they took the exit ramp and left the large five lane artery; he assumed in search of smaller roads and hopefully his final destination. The sign pointing right read Beverly Hills, he'd heard of that, but they turned left towards the ocean. This was down to a two, sometimes three lane road - wide and smooth. The American worship of Mammon had become more evident here. There was shopping on either side selling a variety of goods and services which again were unheard of outside the city. Le Sex Shoppe, Beer & Pool, Rudy's Used Autos - $200 Down, Barbering And Men's Styling, Donny's Cocktails, Adult Theatre, Sin-o-Rama, Hotel Apartments - short term stays, Waterbeds for Sale call Santa Monica 5537. It was a bewildering array of hedonistic delights, which had yet to reach beyond the West Coast.

The car pulled up, the lights on red. An elderly black lady in a flowered summer dress stepped off the curb. She was wearing a white bonnet hat, white gloves and carried a bright yellow and white purse - she looked like she was off to church. She raised her hand in thanks as she crossed the road, to every driver. One of which was a battered pick-up filled with hand tools and covered in dirt; the three men in the front looked like they'd worked hard that day. The driver was at least seventy. Rugged with a lined face and a dirty-white vest; possibly an Okie who'd headed West in the 1930s. He raised a tattered straw hat as a token of respect as the lady passed in front of the truck. Almost the very the last cry of the old, civilized world.

It was now early evening, and the streets were lit up with neon and sodium lights. The taxi came to a halt outside a busy restaurant. The driver turned round in his seat.

"If you haven't eaten, this is a great cantina. Proper Mexican food."

"And you're recommending this because?"

"Hey Mijo, you're Spanish you're gonna love this place"

"Does your friend own it?"

The driver laughed,

"Sure, his name is above the door, Casa Carlos. And be sure to tell him Jesus sent you."

"Will I get a discount then?"

"No but I might!"

Both men were laughing as they drove off into the approaching night. The taxi turned onto Ocean Avenue. Waves were crashing onto the sand. The ocean was pitch black, occasional lights from Santa Monica caught the crests. The air was hot and heavy with just the hint of a light ozone breeze providing relief through the open window. The car pulled up outside The Ocean Hotel; a decrepit turn of the century three-story brick building whose only redeeming feature seemed to be its sea view. It was covered in pink render - most of which appeared to have turned the colour of spoiled meat - a greyer shade of pink. But it had large balconies and a nice view of the pier. The palm trees opposite the hotel swayed in the breeze and there was a quietness about the road; it was that twilight period between evening meal and the creatures of the night awakening from their tombs.

"And here we are."

The car pulled to a halt and Jesus turned in his seat.

"Gracias."

"Don't forget about the restaurant."

"I won't."

"And if you need a car, call me."

"I will."

As well as handing him a card for the restaurant, he handed over a second, plain business card 'Walnut Park Cabs - Ludlow (58) 4118'.

"Are you near the hotel?"

"No, but I'm always in the area."

He waved off the cab, picked up his luggage and checked into the hotel. He sat on the bed in his room.

Now he just needed to wait for the call.

13

Lodestar Operations, Whitehall, London

… 24 hours earlier

"Jack Bradley, I'm with the US Embassy"

A large American in a powder blue suit rose out of his chair and extended a giant hand in his direction. He shook it; firm grip and he detected just a touch of Masonic tendency. A thumb was placed across the third knuckle of his hand as they grasped. Searching, seeking a fellow of the craft.

Bradley was about six foot three with a shock of blonde hair and probably weighed in at around two-fifty. He had an open face and a deep tan. Which first told him this apple-pie eating, flag waving patriot was probably of German or Scandinavian stock from a Midwest farming background. Secondly, it told him this guy had just arrived from the states, and not Chicago, somewhere warm.

He thought he'd try a direct approach.

"So you're a Spook?"

Fraser stood out of his chair, laughing nervously, he said:

"Now then, let's not get bogged down with titles shall we, I mean…"

"It's OK Thomas I got this."

The American raised a hand and smiled with cold eyes.

The Spaniard loved the way Americans insisted on using first name terms with people they hardly knew. On this side of the pond first names where usually reserved for friends and family; and even then, at a push. When Bradley mentioned 'Thomas' he thought *who's that*?

"Actually, I'm with the FBI."

Explains the bad suit, the Spaniard thought.

"I'm on secondment working for a special branch of the organisation in Los Angeles."

Just got off the big silver bird then, explains the tan.

"I can't go into the minutia right now, but we're looking for a private security consultant, a specialist, who's willing to be a part of a project I'm overseeing on the West Coast. And he needs to be a non-US citizen."

OK, the Spaniard thought, so it's illegal and on US soil so the FBI can't officially be part of it. That explains the promise of money.

"Well, I'm happy to listen to you but I'm not going to take part in anything that'll see me locked up in some glass house for the next forty years. That's the military stockade my friend."

The large man smiled and smoothed out the brim on his straw trilby that was resting on the arm of his chair; a bloody straw hat in February, he thought.

"No, no this is a covert operation, but it has the green light from the very top."

"Still Mr … err Bradley, was it?"

"Call me Jack."

"Alright - *Mr Bradley*, what guarantee have I got that I'll not only come out of this richer but also alive and not in some Californian jail?"

"Yes, that's the long and short of it. Look, you seem to be a direct sort of guy, so I'll lay the whole thing out for you. From top to bottom. Then if you like my proposal, we'll take it from there. How's that sound?"

"I'm listening Mr Bradley, and I may even be taking notes."

Santa Monica Beach, 1971 … almost midnight

He's walking through thick SE Asian jungle; it's hot, unbelievably hot and humid. The moon illuminates everything around him, the leaves, the vines, palm fronds look like they're all coated in silver plate. The whole scene is shrouded in jungle steam; he can hear his own breath - it's short and sharp. A twig snaps to the right of him. He stops, dead in his tracks, turning towards the sound. Was it a CT (Chinese Terrorist) or just a Malayan farmer; is he about to face a Tiger or is it just a civet cat foraging for food? The whole jungle falls silent, nothing and then the explosion.

His world is filled with fire, all around him. He's running, faster, faster. Now he's back on the streets of Kuala Lumpur. He sees the black Wolseley car overturned in the road. The old sedan is leaking oil and fuel, and it's on fire. She's lying on the ground trapped underneath. There's blood on her white dress. Her head turns toward him, eyes suddenly open. The world is filled with screaming, it's her, his wife … He shouts,

"Noooo…"

He woke with a start, jumping up in bed drenched in sweat. His black hair plastered on his head and his vest soaked through. It took him a while to work out where he was. OK America, West Coast, California, it's not 1956. Alright OK, she's still dead but I'm alive, for now. He calmed himself down, breathing deep, concentrating, using meditation techniques he learnt in SE Asia. Close your eyes, focus on only the now, take a deep inward breath, let it out very, very slowly.

"Just focus on the *here* and *now*,"

He could hear the old Buddhist monk say. And he repeated it to himself in his mind.

The memory of his wife's death was strongly imprinted and a difficult memory to scrub. She was working as a nurse in a hospital in Kuala Lumpur, the Malay capital, and he was going to meet her for lunch. He was back for two weeks on 'r and r' from the civil war in the jungle; named the Malayan Emergency as not to admit it was an actual war. They'd planned to lunch at a tea house near his hotel. He was waiting at a table outside and saw the car draw up, there were a few nurses inside and a senior surgeon, who was driving. That's when the car bomb went off, blowing the car into the air, flipping it and it landed on its roof killing all inside instantly.

He closed his eyes and began again to use this ancient breathing technique to calm himself, concentrating on the breath. After a few minutes he opened his eyes again, checking the watch by his bed. The illuminated hands showed just after midnight. He climbed out of bed towards the half-open hotel window, enjoying the sea breeze as it wafted into the room. Looking out across the ocean, he thought: this room is dreadful, but the view is five star. He could see across the whole bay from Malibu in the north to Torrance in the South. Not that he knew then what he was looking at; it was just pretty coastline. The moonlight caught the top of the pier, illuminating the roller-coaster, showing the age of its construction; another antique from a bygone age, not unlike himself.

He lit a small half-smoked cigar lying in the ashtray beside the bed, exhaling deeply, again. He can hear arguing outside on the seafront. A truck has caught the side of a large Chevy sedan; this was the sound of the bang, and maybe the scream, that woke him. Well, he won't sleep now; jetlagged, he threw on some pants and a shirt and went out.

He turned left out of the hotel and passed the accident. There was an ambulance, two police cars, a huddle of concerned/nosey bystanders and a blonde girl sat on the curb crying: obviously the screamer in his dream. There was glass everywhere and a bloodied man being helped into the back of one of the ambulances. Seems organised, back home in London you'd be better off making your way to the hospital than waiting for help, you could be out in the cold for a long time.

Walking along the seafront he started to shiver, his thin cotton shirt and dress trousers from his suit did not keep out the sea breeze. It may be a warm February in LA but after you've lived in SE Asia on and off for most of your adult life everywhere is cold. He made a mental note to pick-up some more suitable gear tomorrow; this is starting to look like a slightly longer operation than was first anticipated; no word yet from the contact. Breaking into a gentle jog along the seafront to keep warm, he headed south towards Venice beach trying to kill off jetlag and bad memories.

He stood illuminated by the sign from the 7/11 convenience store. Still trying to believe he'd actually bought a soda, and something called a 'Baby Ruth' chocolate bar at 12.43am. This was unheard of anywhere else on the planet. In London everywhere was closed by 5pm, Asia maybe 7pm and in the Middle East, well there wasn't anything to buy whatever the time of day it was. Buoyed by the refreshing drink that was Coca Cola and the sickly but sweet chocolate, he began to stroll along the seafront taking in the sights and sounds that were Venice Beach.

He firstly noticed rubbish everywhere, all over the pathway, beer bottles, food wrappers, even bits of misplaced clothing; all coated with a generous dusting of sand from the beach which was right next to the boardwalk. As he walked further, he could see the reason for all the detritus. A rock band were packing up - obviously after an impromptu open-air concert on the beach, roadies were de-rigging gear, garbage men were collecting rubbish and dumping it into trash cans and all around were littered bodies in various states of consciousness. From drop-down-dead drunks to groups of intense college students in circles passing round a joint. The flotsam and jetsam of the night also appeared to have washed up on the boardwalk as he made his way along the shoreline. A proper mix of the eclectic characters that had been drawn to this part of the land of the free. Hippies smoking weed, homeless pushing shopping carts, Mexican women selling cheap toys, Vietnam vets in wheelchairs with placards, a group of Hells Angels stood around a collection of amazing motorcycles, beautiful girls with blonde hair and acoustic guitars. One of whom was blowing bubbles into the air, to the delight of her friends; they were reflecting the lights from the pier. Weirdly an old white man in a summer dress covered in small flowers walked along holding hands with an overweight middle-aged black prostitute.

The air was warm with just a slight breeze coming in from the Pacific; he'd begun to heat up. The hubble and bubble of people around him made him feel slightly more human; despite the fact that the task ahead of him would be dehumanising. Although considering his background as a solder and mercenary it came with the territory. At least this job was for the greater good and not just the money. At least that's what he kept telling himself.

He came to crossroads and was about to head back to Santa Monica and his delightful pink hotel when he heard music coming from a very small shop on the corner. It was captivating, Spanish flamenco guitar but with something more; a kind of rumba beat behind it. Certainly, very different from anything he'd heard since Spain. The shop it emanated from looked like a shack for selling fishing bait and tackle. It was all sun-bleached driftwood and faux nautical lanterns. He made his way past a number of the night crawlers and walked inside - the door was open. To his surprise it was a record shop, just a bit more Los Angeles than Carnaby Street, and it was huge once you got inside. There were racks and racks of LPs, and a few hardcore musicologists were fingering their way through album after album. Like the hungry seeking food or drug addicts just that next fix. You could see the joy on someone's face when they picked a newly discovered favourite and took it out to admire the cover, let alone hear the music.

That enchanting music continued to fill the room; the music had broken into a full flamenco instrumental track. It reminded him of his time in Madrid, living amongst the poorest on the street but hearing the greatest music from the

Andalusian flamenco guitaristas who played for pennies outside the city's restaurants. He approached the counter of the shop where a young girl was cataloguing a stack of LPs.

"Hello, I was, erm just wondering what this music is?"

She looked up from her notes, smiling; she had jet black hair and large dark green eyes.

"Ahh, you have taste. This is new straight off the plane from Madrid. It's a Spanish guitarist called Paco de Lucia, the album's called Fuente y Caudal, its means…"

"I know what it means, source and flow"

He could hear her slight Spanish accent."

"Tu hable Espanol Señor?"

"Si, I am Spanish," he replied grinning.

She tossed her shoulder length hair, laughing and wagged a finger at him, replying in Spanish,

"Then sir you should already know Paco De Lucia; he's a star in Spain."

"Well, I've been out of the country for a few years."

"But he's been a star since the mid-sixties."

"I've been away for longer."

There was a long pause between the two of them. She recognised something was being unsaid and for a moment they just stared at each other, in a trance-like state.

He smiled and broke the silence.

"Are you from Mexico?"

"No Nicaragua, I've come to the US to study. The universities back at home can only take me so far. And to pay for that I sell records. How about you? You're Spanish but you're not coming from Spain? You sound English."

"Good guess, yes London. It's where I live now; I'm in Los Angeles on business."

"Really? One AM in the morning in Venice Beach is a strange place for a businessman."

He laughed as Paco De Lucia hammered off and on his acoustic guitar, blasting the speakers in the shop.

"Yes, you're right I'm here by accident. My hotel is up at Santa Monica, and I walked here because I'm suffering from jetlag. I'm amazed your shop is open."

She looked back at him, leaning on the counter. Arching her back very slightly, she whispered,

"Well believe me it's not by choice. My dumb boss thinks we can make a killing by opening late when there's a concert at South Beach Park."

"And is he right?"

He looked around the now empty shop.

"Well, you're the first person to ask me about the music in the past two hours. I've spent my time going through inventory, smoking cigarettes and chasing away bums."

"Would I make it a more successful night if I bought this record?"

"Erm, I believe you would. But this is a Spanish import, so - it's very expensive."

"Price is not a problem. This is great music; it reminds me of being a kid in Madrid."

She smiled, carefully took the record off the player, placed it into its sleeve and wrapped it in a large paper bag.

"You are now the proud owner of our last copy of this record and, I've decided. my last customer."

She switched off the main lights behind the counter and began to ask patrons to exit the building. When they were alone, she lit a cigarette.

He paid for the record and smiling said,

"I have a small problem?"

"Si?"

"I don't have a record player."

She smiled, looked skyward, laughed and clapped her hands together.

"Maybe we can solve that problem. How about a drink tomorrow night at my place?"

"Tequila?"

"No I'm Nicaraguan not Mexican *idiota*. Rum - and I'm buying."

Santa Monica Beach - Morning

He was dreaming of walking along Venice Beach in the early hours, the breeze from the ocean cool on his skin. He was drinking rum looking into those dark eyes, the music was flamenco, the beat was rumba … and then there was a ringing, louder and louder.

He awoke with a jolt, the black Bakelite phone on the nightstand vibrating the glass of water next to it. Although it was early Californian sun streamed through the shutters and into the room. He rubbed his eyes and tried to remember where he was. He knew. He picked up the receiver.

"Get ready."

The deep, dry voice just breathed the words as if they already knew the power they held.

"For what?"

"We're gonna take a ride."

"Go where?"

"… shopping, of course."

The voice on the other end broke into a small chuckle. Then nothing, just a click and the sound of dial tone. He figured he would be getting a visitor; this was about the job he was here to do. He needed to get washed and ready before the mystery voice turned up.

It was just after eight and he was drinking the last of his black coffee, provided by the hotel's front desk. The place might be a flop house, he mused, but there's nowhere in England - not even The Ritz - where the reception desk lays on free coffee for its residents. He arrived downstairs fifteen minutes previous and asked the small balding concierge where he could get a hot drink. The response was - help yourself to our coffee, pointing to a coffee maker full of the black stuff sitting on the front desk. He was already two and a half cups in. An ancient bell chimed above the front door, one of those on the end of a spring from the 1920s, and a man walked in.

Medium to large build and in his mid-thirties he sported a small moustache and a shiny sharkskin silk suit, just a little too tight and a little out of date. He wore a small grey hat, which matched the suit and the jet-black Wayfarer sunglasses, which matched his skin. There was very little of either the gentleman or the priest about him. He looked like, what he probably was: a bent cop and this look said *Don't Fuck With Me* - very loudly.

"You ready?"

Was the only introduction he offered.

"Where are we going?"

"You'll see. Come on, we gotta go."

He held the front door open and beckoned the Spaniard through.

The unrelenting West Coast sun beat down on the car as they cruised along the highway; back on the 405 heading south. The Saturday morning traffic was light. And the journey not unpleasant, the ride was super smooth in a silver two-door mid-60s Chevy Impala. The driver lit a cigarette with a Zippo and exhaled the white smoke out of his open window.

"First time in LA?" the driver enquired

"First time in California" he replied.

They cruised past Mar Vista on one side and Culver City on the other. A local station was pumping out Motown on the stereo and thankfully the aircon was turned way up. He turned to look at the driver

"So, are you a G man?"

"Do I look like a motherfucking Fed?"

"Like I said, first time here so how the hell would I know?"

The driver turned to him and for the first time smiled and laughed.

"OK now I know you're the man for the job. Yeah, I bet a motherfucker like you's seen all sorts of shit."

"All sorts. So, what's your story?"

"Not much I'm just a gopher man; I go for this, and I go for that. Look I'm a private operative who does the occasional babysitting work for Uncle Sam."

"Like Sam Spade?"

"Careful who you're calling a spade, pendejo."

"That's not what I meant."

"I know hombre, I'm just fucking with you."

The Spaniard looked skyward and shook his head. The detective smiled, offering a cigarette. He declined and took out a half smoked thin lancero cigar accepting the offer of the Zippo lighter. Not a great thing to do with a Cuban cigar: pollute it by using a petrol lighter, but he figured it'd make for some sort of bond with his new contact. He exhaled the thin stream of Cuban smoke, mirroring his driver and blowing it out of the window across towards Inglewood.

"Where are we going? And what are we shopping for?"

"Well, where we're going, my Latino brother, is the ghetto and what we is shopping for is hardware."

"*Latino*, no I'm Spanish not Latino"

"You's an Espanol in Spain but here my man you's Latino"

Ok, he thought, don't press the point, this guy's far too low on the food chain to push the point. But it confused him that in Europe he was a Caucasian but here he was Latino. He took another hit from the small cigar as the car turned off the 405 onto the Century Freeway.

The buildings were becoming more residential and more dilapidated. And when they exited the highway, he understood what the driver had meant by 'the ghetto': the housing was all run down, there were vacant lots which looked like they'd been firebombed, a sign on a store read 'Wheelers TV & Radio - serving Watts since 1954'. And everyone, almost exclusively was either Black or Spanish.

"Wow, I've fought in better looking warzones."

The detective smiled, lighting another cigarette

"Welcome to Charcoal Alley."

"Why's it called that?"

"Race riots back in the Sixties. The brothers decided to burn that motherfucker down and all those hopped up negros left was charcoal. What a fucking mess, you ain't gonna find no white son-of-a-bitch is gonna burn down his house 'cause he's pissed."

The car pulled up to the curb on a little side street just off Wilmington. The street was made up of small one-story concrete houses that looked like they'd been thrown up in a hurry; and never maintained since. Two girls and a small boy were playing tag in the sunshine but apart from that it was a quiet day in South Central.

The front door of the house was weathered, someone had painted it a long time ago and now twenty summers later the paint was peeling off revealing the dry sun-bleached wood beneath. Cracks has started to appear and not just on the paint. The PI loudly knocked three times, and a series of clunks and rattles responded, signifying someone was very worried about home security. A giant of a man in a dirty white t-shirt and old army fatigues opened the door. The PI stepped up.

"We're here about the hardware."

The large black man smiled and pushed open an old, ripped screen door.

"Then *you* better come in."

30

Lodestar Operations, Whitehall, London

… Thursday 4th February 1971

The FBI's Jack Bradley strolled across the room and helped himself to another drink. The clink of ice was followed by the click of an electric lighter as he lit another cigarette. Exhaling Connecticut's finest he turned and walked back across the room.

"You see that what we need is your military skills to help us keep California free from the rising tide of organised crime. My boss Mr Hoover is a big fan of that."

From behind his expensive desk, his usual hiding place, Fraser piped up.

"Yes, I've heard he has a bee in his bonnet about the Mob."

"Yep, that and the Commies; he's a real hard ass about those."

Bradley took a swig of the second scotch and wiped his mouth with the back of that large hand.

"Now this job is a little hush, hush, if you get my drift. We can't recruit stateside as any loose threads could lead back to the Bureau and we can't have that. I need a foreign professional; a man who can fly in get the job done and fly out again."

He leaned towards the Spaniard.

"Through a colleague at Langley I'd been given Lodestar's details in London. They've been involved in private military actions for decades and Mr Fraser here thought you'd be perfect for the job. You're ex-military, a sniper, a former cop and these days a gun for hire. You fit the bill."

He opened his hands waiting for a response.

"So, what'd ya say fella?"

Both men stared at the Spaniard intently, eyes smiling, almost willing him to say yes. He rose from the chair, took his mackintosh coat from the hat stand and walked towards the door and stopped dead. Turning back towards them he smiled.

"Twenty years gentlemen I've been fighting for King, country and whichever Third World autocrat will pay me. And I may be a soldier and a mercenary but one thing I am not and that is a fucking killer for hire."

Alarmed the fat FBI man waved his hands in front of his sizable frame.

"No, no that's not what this is about, this is a political move by my country to…"

"Save your breath Mr Bradley. I'm not a gun for hire, not to you anyway." He reached for the door handle.

"Wait, wait, wait. Just hang on a goddamn minute here."

Bradley loosened his tie and swept back his thinning blond hair. He mumbled,

"Ok, Ok, we'll double the fee."

He turned to Fraser who looked perplexed then nodded in the affirmative. Then louder

"…*we'll double the fee!*"

The Spaniard paused, gripping intensely the brass door handle, which would lead him out of the building and this situation. Images of past lives flashed before him: Spain, The Far East and England. He'd sacrificed much of his morality as both a soldier and privateer and this could be his road to financial redemption. He was living on a merger army pension and hadn't worked as a military contractor for almost two years since Oman and cash was getting tight. This could be a last chance to retire from this life as a gun for hire, pay off the mortgage on his small house and choose another career - one with less consequences. It was an extreme act but maybe a necessary one. His decision had been made; he relaxed his grip on the door handle. He turned back to Bradley.

"For $100,000 Mr Bradley I will be your assassin. But on two conditions. I want a full pardon from the US government signed in advance. So, if I get caught all this will just go away. And I want half the cash up front."

"Hey, I don't have that sort of…"

"Say yes Mr Bradley, yes or I walk away now."

Bradley looked at Fraser who shrugged,

"I don't think he's giving you a choice Jack."

Bradley walked away and slumped into some of Lodestar's expensive leather chairs. He looked deflated and raised a hand in acceptance.

"OK, yes, yes you got it."

Los Angeles Interstate 405

They motored down the highway in the giant Chevy Impala - it looked like a silver shark from space that someone had decorated with chrome for Christmas. He relaxed back into his seat and let the PI concentrate on driving. Window wound right down; his hand played with the slip stream in time with the regular beats of the tamping lies on the interstate. Now they resounded to the beat of rumba and flamenco in his head 'bbrr-duh, brr-duh, brru-duh-duh-duh-duh'. Again, he thought of the music in that shop on Venice beach - Paco De Lucia. He thought of the girl he would be meeting tonight with the green Spanish eyes and the black Indian hair. He mused over their assignation and stared wistfully into the distance, the sun was sinking low again, a beautiful tropical sunset framed with the occasional palm tree. It reminded him of the Causeway between Singapore and Malaya. He was disturbed out of his daydream by the PI.

"Hey, you happy with the fusil, Ese?"

The PI was smiling at him from the driver's seat, cigarette in mouth, looking directly at him over his sunglasses.

"Si, el rile es muy bien y tu Espanol es mierda idiota!"

"Hey, hey I don't know precisely what you said man, but I don't take kindly to no Latino insults. Look you got yourself a great weapon man, Remington 700 - it'll kill all the ways up to a thousand yards."

34

He'd watched the giant gun dealer in the army fatigues explain the ins and outs of the weapon in the back room of the dilapidated house. The whole set up looked like some sort of used arms depot in the Third World. Windows were blacked out and bare bulbs hung with flypaper from the ceiling. Handguns lined the walls, wooden boxes of rifles were piled up on top of each other, some worryingly in standard army green and sporting printed lettering - US Ordnance. On the desk was a disassembled machine gun surrounded by the accoutrements of gun maintenance - oil cans, rags, screwdrivers, and other assorted gun paraphernalia. The place smelt of sweat, oil and cordite. The cordite came from the cellar where there was an improvised range of sorts. It was a long thin tunnel extending from the house's original cellar underneath the garden, lit by bulbs a paper target was placed at the end in front of standard army issue sandbags. In fact, the whole place smelt like a sort of unofficial special ops set up. A safe house where weapons could be purchased for undercover use only. And when neighbours complained about the gun shots emanating from the basement, bribed local patrolmen simply ignored them.

He'd descended the cellar and shot the rifle numerous times, it cycled correctly, didn't jam, didn't misfire and most importantly of all for the job in hand it was accurate. When they finally decided to purchase the weapon the gun runner had carefully cleaned the barrel, the stock, handle and trigger before placing it into a large canvas bag. Which had, at the time, seemed an unusual act of respect but now as he sat it the car on the way back to his hotel felt like a felon getting rid of prints. This didn't fill him with confidence.

The Ford pulled up outside his hotel and he retrieved the rifle from the trunk. The PI leaned outside the driver's window.

"We'll be seeing you later my man."

Before he had time to answer the car sped off down Ocean Avenue in the direction of downtown LA. He stared across the beach as the ocean started to roll in and the waves crashed on the shore. The scene was light in glistering gold by the setting sun. Then, to no one but himself, he muttered

"Time and tide, time and tide."

La Casa Carlos Santa Monica - that night.

When his wife died the Spaniard mourned for days that had turned into months. He been given some R&R from the service but to be honest the military had kept him occupied and his mind distracted from the trauma. It was the 1950s, they were only just accepting shell shock or PTSD as a concept. He'd been given some leave by his commanding officer and headed north out of Kuala Lumpur on an old motorbike. He'd passed through Perak and Taiping and finally come to a halt at Butterworth. All three were similar Malayan towns, busy marketplaces, bustling nightlife and full of troops searching out CT insurgents. At Butterworth he'd caught the local ferry and after showing the crewman his military identification he'd been ushered aboard for the crossing to Penang Island. It was a small Singapore of the north and had been occupied by the British for almost two hundred years. He was hoping to find peace and solace in the quiet Regency streets of George Town and amongst the lush jungles of the island.

His Commanding Officer had recommended staying at The Eastern and Oriental Hotel along the seafront. The grizzled veteran from the war in Burma had laughed.

"Hot and cold-water old boy, lovely long seafront and most importantly of all, the owner imports bloody good Scotch."

The colonel was right about the Scotch and the hot water, but the Spaniard had been to the hotel before with his late wife. The seafront view across the Penang Strait drew him in every evening. He sat in a rattan chair drinking himself into a coma staring out across sea as dusk fell and the purple, red and yellow colours reached out across the sky. A sky it would have been impossible, or at least unrealistic, for an artist to truly capture.

It was this same unbelievable, surreal sky he looked at across the Santa Monica Bay from his table at Casa Carlos more than fifteen years later. It was just after six on a Saturday night the place was comfortably busy. The staff weren't bored waiting to fill covers but were having fun serving the clientele. Likewise, the customers were able to choose their tables, and no one had, as yet, been placed by the kitchen door or the toilet; notorious locations for the physically unattractive, the rude and all latecomers. Tonight, everyone at Casa Carlos were all smiles.

It was a beautifully set out restaurant, more elegant eatery than Mexican cantina. There were booths set back against the wall for more discreet diners and the whole of the restaurant opened up with, large glass doors, to a huge, covered terrace; letting customers enjoy the night air. There were small lanterns on each table and rustic Hispanic antiques from mirrors and candelabras to swords and old wagon wheels adorning the walls. It reminded him of an upscale tourist spot back home in say Malaga or Marbella. Just *Spanish* enough for the customers without chickens being decapitated and small dogs running around one's feet. Not that that bothered him. Some of the best meals he'd had had been prepared in kitchens with dirt floors by a cook with one pan and one gas hob who probably spent half their life chasing away the rats.

The customers were a mixture of well-to-do Hispanics, the odd college professor type and quite a few long-haired youths of both sexes. In fact, the fashion for hirsuteness was becoming the norm these days for. He'd even started to grow his own jet black hair below the collar; he still slicked it back with hair oil but it was becoming decidedly bohemian. He liked it; it made a change from the short back and sides of the British military. He smoothed back his hair and stared out across the bay. The last of the sun being extinguished in the dark blue stillness of the Pacific. The waitress brought him a small glass of blended scotch with a single ice cube; he allowed himself only one cube. After all he was still a former British officer and as his CO used to say

"The Americans love ice in their whisky, but you've got to be careful my boy. Any old piss will taste good with ice in it!"

He'd booked the table for seven o'clock and was looking forward to his night with the beautiful girl from the record shop. The Nicaraguan with the Spanish green eyes.

A hand suddenly grasped his shoulder and for just a moment he went to drop his weight and reach for the hand in question to pivot the owner across the table. It was instinctual but right at the last moment he turned to see a slightly wide-eyed Jesus, his smiling 'gypsy' taxi driver, from Walnut Park.

"Hey sorry Senor I didn't mean to shock you. I was just pleased to see you here."

The man had stepped back from the table hands open in supplication.

"Hello, sorry, yes you startled me a bit there. Como Estas?

"Estoy bien, garcias amigo, gracias"

Jesus was still dressed from top to toe in black but had given up on his usual yellow driving glasses. He smiled a broad gold-toothed smile.

"I knew you'd come here, la comida es excellente. Try the octopus it's heaven. And make sure you mention me to Carlos you'll get a discount."

The driver handed over another Walnut Taxis business card and turned to walk away.

"And I imagine you'll get a free meal out of this?"

"Por supuesto Señor," he said turning back.

"We all have to eat!" he smiled and walked away to chat to the owner by the bar.

The restaurant suddenly seemed to grow quiet, or at least this is what his perception was, as she walked in through the main entrance. Her long black Taino Indian hair shaped her beautiful face and offset by two piercing green eyes. All five-foot-four of her was clad in a simple white dress that clung to her petite but proportioned frame. She had the curving breasts and pert behind that's genetically present across Latin America. The mix of native Indian, the Spanish and Mediterranean conquistadors and more than a heavy dose of West African courtesy of the slave trade. This made for some of the most beautiful people on the planet. She was wearing a classic silver and amber necklace. As if in slow motion she made her way towards him, receiving admiring glances from customers and staff alike.

"Ahh Maylin. Como estas, Maylin? Estas preocia."

One of the waitresses had recognised her and had gone to greet her, holding her hands and stepping back to get the full picture.

"Tienes una cita? Where is the lucky man?"

She pointed directed to him and smiled.

The cheeky waitress whisked her over, smiling at him.

"This one looks good. Buena suerte"

She winked. He stood up.

"I'm sure we will be lucky Senorita. Muchas gracias."

The waitress, realising the man understood Spanish, laughed with embarrassment running back off to the kitchen. He stood up offering her a seat.

"So your name in Maylin and she is a friend?"

"Just another expat Nicaraguan trying to make her way in LA."

"Your name, it's Chinese for beautiful jade, Mei Lin. Are you named after your eyes?"

"The day I was born my father said, look at those, there is only one name we can give her."

They were a brilliant green, full of life, dancing with energy reflecting the lights of the restaurant. He complemented her

"You look beautiful."

"And you too."

He was wearing his thin linen suit with a new silk shirt in powder blue he'd bought from a boutique near the hotel. He smiled

"Can a man be beautiful?"

"Oh yes, there are many beautiful men."

She sat down across from him.

"Now you know my name but what about yours."

"All in good time, all in good time. And I brought my long player record with me."

He reached under the table producing the Paco De Lucia album he'd bought from her in the early hours of the morning. She took it from him.

"If you're very lucky we can listen to it later back at my house. Right now I need to eat, I am ravenous - muy hambriento."

They ordered from the menu. A good bottle of Californian Merlot and made their way through starters, mains and finally desert. There were plates of octopus, as recommended by Jesus the taxi tout, traditional Mexican seafood dishes, steak, tamales all with plenty of spicy *salsa picante.* They talked and talked. Of her work in the record shop, her studying International Relations at UCLA and her large family in

Nicaraguan, where her parents owned a cigar factory.

"My father is a traditional businessman; he won't entertain the idea of modern socialism."

"I spent years fighting communists in the jungles of SE Asia. I have some sympathy with him"

She looked across at him sternly. He quickly countered.

"But I believe both capitalism and social welfare can co-exist. We have it in Britain."

She laughed,

"I was testing you; of course, there needs to be responsible democracy."

"Did I pass the test?"

"The jury is still out" she smiled and laughed.

When they'd both finished, he reached for the bill, she stopped him.

"Hey, let's split la cuenta"

"I'll pick this one up, you get the next. And besides, I believe you have a bottle of famous Nicaraguan rum at home that I'd love to try. Plus, you promised to play my new record."

"That rum does sound good. Maybe as good as the record."

Outside the restaurant, underneath an overhanging tree, two men sat in an unremarkable dark green car. One black, one Hispanic. One smoking a cigarette, the other not.

"Does he know the full extent of the operation?"

"Not yet, but he's pretty clever. He'll work it out."

"You think?"

"Yes, I'm sure."

"I hope you're right for his sake; otherwise, this guy is one dead motherfucker."

Venice Beach, Los Angeles - Late

They'd taken a long walk along the seafront to get to her place. Walking hand in hand and enjoying the quiet; just the warm wind and the crashing sound of waves. Her house was situated just off the beach in Venice, round the back of a line of shops. It was a small white, but faded, two-bedroom bungalow and most importantly of all it faced Santa Monica Bay. They climbed the old wooden stairs, passing metal wind chimes and a small tattered blue and white flag. He pointed at the flag.

"Nicaragua?"

Maylin smiled and looked skyward

"Oh that's my crazy roommate - she's obsessed with the idea of revolution at home."

"And you?"

"Me? Not so much."

They entered the small two-bedroomed house. It was sparsely furnished but obviously well-kept and quite pretty. There were a few posters on the walls. 'Newport '69' - he recognised none of the pop performers. War? Jethro Tull? And he thought the Taj Mahal was a building not a black musician. There was a poster for Monterey Jazz Festival 1970 - he recognised Duke Ellington and saxophonist Sonny Stitt, much more his era. The jazz references sparked a memory of the dancehalls of Singapore and KL; local bands would cover the latest bebop sounds of the day and from overseas some great acts from Ronnie Scott's Club in London and the occasional superstar. In 1956 it was the king of swing himself Benny Goodman who played a packed-out show in Kula Lumpur,

Maylin turned towards him.

"Lost in thought."

"Sorry yes I was looking at the posters and remembered seeing some great jazz performances in the past."

"Yes, I'm the jazz fan; Josefina my roomy is more into the pop and rock scene."

"Your roomy?"

"Yes, oh right I forgot you're Spanish. She's my friend I share the house with."

He smiled she pronounced the name Josefina with a 'H' the way every good Spanish speaker does. It'd just been a while since he'd heard it. He missed the sound of Spanish voices.

"No rock and roll for you then?"

"No, it's just a little too noisy for me; all I can hear is chaos."

"I think that's what they used to say about jazz!"

They both laughed and she led him over to the record player

"You put this on and I'll get that rum", handing him the record.

He placed the disc carefully on the turntable blowing away any excess dust and hairs. He then started the machine at 33rmp and carefully placed the stylus onto the record. There was a click and then slowly the Spanish flamenco guitar sounds of this virtuoso began to drift out of the speakers. It was a nice stereo; a Thorns turntable with a forty-watt amp and a beautiful silver radio turner. All set-in faux wood.

"This is a very nice stereo." he called to Maylin in the kitchen.

There was a Spanish language newspaper next to the record player, *La Movilizasion Republicana*. He picked it up and glanced through the some of the articles; the front-page lead with 'Founder In Pan American Talks'. There was a picture of a small Nicaraguan man in glasses smiling.

She reappeared with two glasses of dark rum.

"Oh yes that newspaper's Josefina's, her family is very well off so they pay for the record player, but her politics are much more *of the people*. Amazing how the more committed you are to the socialist cause the more likely your parents are part of the establishment. It's like the first rebellion is against Mama and Papa."

She handed him a glass of rum and in unison they drank. He smiled at her

"This is pretty good stuff."

"It's the best - Flor de Caña Extra Anejo; seven years old. Which means its…"

Suddenly the room began to shake, ornaments fell from shelves, books likewise and pictures dropped from walls smashing glass. The front door trembled like someone was trying to break in and the lights flickered. It lasted no more than ten seconds but felt like a lifetime. He pulled her towards him, holding her close.

"Earthquake?"

"Mierda! Yes, I fucking hate those things. Back home we have the same. That was a little one. It either means there's a big one somewhere else or a big quake is on its way."

He held her tight and pulled her closer, their lips almost touching, their eyes looking deeply into each other, their pulses had quickened.

"We better make the most of the time we have left then."

"Dios Mio"

She whispered, they kissed.

He was standing on the deck at the front of the little wooden house looking towards the Pacific, it was late or possibly early, maybe 4am. Lights glistened as far as the eye could see, either side of the valley and down towards the black ocean. Mist drifted across the sea caught by the light from the moon; it was in its first or third quarter - half in shape. He'd been too busy to remember whether a full moon was due or had already passed. When he was a child, he remembered staring out across his father's fields in the Asturias countryside, mist hugging hedgerows and the silence of the night. There were less lights then than now, but one could still taste the salt in the air from the sea, the ozone pervaded everything and told you that out there was a beast who was more powerful than any empire that'd ever existed. It humbled him, but in a good way, it let him know that here on land, power was fleeting.

She was still asleep, looking perfect, in a post-coital slumber - the moonlight highlighting her perfect figure even as she lay prone. He'd tied a sheet from their bed around his waist and made his way outside so as not to disturb her. He wore it like a sarong; the way he'd worn them back in the jungle and occasionally when visiting the homes of his men or a Malay Mosque. He'd properly adopted their culture when he lived in Peninsular Malaya and Borneo. He liked their way of living and the way they had accepted him with ease. His commanding officers had thought this was a little too much and that he'd gone 'native' but his ability to blend in with local culture gave him numerous professional victories. He worked through the ranks eventually working as an officer in counterintelligence.

He lit the remains of an old cigar and leaned on the wooden balcony of the porch. In the distance he could hear music and people, maybe a street away. Voices, the sound of jazz, yes Dizzy Gilespie, bebop, like it was still 1957 and everything was 'cool daddy-o' but as he drained the last of the rum from his glass, he realised everything most certainly was not.

The Hilton, Downtown Los Angeles.

Light poured into the dark hotel room from the hall as a large figure entered and then closed the door. He kept the light off and went over the expansive window and opened both the curtain and the nets to let the lights of the city illuminate the room without the need to be seen from the streets below. The man lit a cigarette suddenly illuminating his large face and briefly revealing himself as the FBI's Jack Bradley.

Bradley was exhausted, his flight from Washington had been delayed and by the time he'd landed at LAX almost all the taxis were gone. He looked like he'd been through the ringer. His powder blue suit was wrinkled, his striped Brookes Brothers tie was loose, his hair was a mess, and his face had a hangdog look about it. His massive bulk was illuminated again when he opened the mini bar door, taking out a beer and peanuts. He feed himself the snacks and drank the refreshing beer straight from the bottle as he unplugged the hotel phone, throwing it onto one of the twin beds. From a leather bag he produced another phone, similar to the hotel's own but with a number of extra switches and buttons; including one which read 'Engage for Secret'. He plugged it in and dialled a very long number.

"Hello, yes, it's me. Don't talk I'm in a hotel. Switching to scramble next."

There as a slight pause as he moved dials and engaged buttons.

"Hello yes, no terrible journey from DC; I'm exhausted. OK yes, I know the line's not one hundred percent secure that's alright. I won't be long."

Another pause as he listened to instructions.

"Yes, yes tell the old man that the target will be in position within the next few days following the conference talks and that our man is ready to go."

"He's got the weapon; he's enjoying a little R&R right now but believe me he's ready for the operation."

The fat American sat on one of the twin beds and lit a cigarette, inhaling the smoke deeply, he cricked his neck from one side to the other. The voice on the other end of the phone sounded robotic and metallic; maybe it was the scrambler unit or maybe it just revealed the true nature of the people in Washington he was working for.

"The chief is counting on you to make sure the job is completed cleanly and in time. Can you guarantee that Bradley, can you promise us that?"

Bradley looked skyward as if in frustration and seeking divine intervention.

"Yes, yes of course it's all gonna happen, just as we planned."

Silence.

"Just get it done Bradley."

Then a click and nothing, not even ringtone. Bradley exhaustedly hung up. He took a drag from his cigarette

"Fuck me, you sons of bitches."

And with that he threw the empty beer bottle into the trash and collapsed on the bed.

Outside the Hilton, underneath a streetlight, two men sat in an unremarkable dark green car. One black, one Hispanic. One smoking a cigarette, the other not. Both were wearing headphones. The Hispanic man turned to the black man, who was adjusting the dials on a portable reel-to-reel Tandberg tape machine.

"Did we get all of that?"

"Nothing from the hotel phone, he scrambled that; so, he could've been talking to Elvis, Jesus or the Dali Lama for all we know. But I bugged the painting, the light and the curtains. I got plenty. Enough to convict."

"OK then it appears that this operation has been green light."

The men smiled and nodded at each other.

"Looks that way my man."

52

Venice Beach, Los Angeles - Early

Sunday morning in this part of LA was a quiet affair, well at least at 6am it was. He'd woken an hour ago - jetlag striking yet again; you were either deadly tired in the middle of the day or wide awake at midnight. It was God's way of telling man that we shouldn't really be travelling across the earth this fast but in the twentieth century it was increasingly the norm. As a child in Spain no one travelled, no one relocated, everyone was born, lived and died in Asturias. As far as anyone could remember everyone he'd known as a child was from that cold northern part of *España*. That'd certainly changed in the last thirty years; you could catch a jet in London and be in Moscow by lunchtime, you didn't have to take a couple of months to get to Australia (from anywhere) and there was a man on the moon, or so we've been told. His answer to jetlag was usually half a bottle of good Scotch but at this hour that seemed a little excessive, even for LA.

He'd showered and kissed Maylin gently on the head, leaving hot coffee on the stove. She was dead to the world and mumbled something about 'catching him later' before her head hit the pillow and she was back in the arms of Morpheus.

The promise of a glorious day was signalled on the horizon as a small dull orange glow spreading across the top of the ocean beneath a cloudless sky. The streets were dead, and his only friends were seagulls and litter; who together almost seemed to be dancing around him as he strolled down the boardwalk. Just behind the first few hundred feet of buildings facing the ocean was the occasional oil derrick, which seemed to be a strange place to drill for the black gold. Beach resorts and oil fields were incongruous bedfellows but the old man, on the front desk at his hotel, Overton, had told him they'd discovered oil back in the 1920s and after the Wall Street crash of '29 it was the only thing that saved California from the Depression; well, that and the oranges. There had at one time been hundreds all up and down the coast. Now they were almost all gone with just a few derricks left to suck out the last remains of the fuel that keeps the big machine going. He felt like those old oil fields, almost exhausted dry and waiting to be decommissioned.

This last job he'd agreed to do would set him up for the rest of his life. He could pay off the mortgage on his dilapidated house by the river in London and live a slightly more extravagant retirement than his meagre army pension would allow. As long as it was invested wisely. He was pondering this thought as he made his way off the beach and towards his hotel.

Suddenly a large car pulled up in front of him and two huge men with badly cut hair and suits to match jumped out. He span round to run off down the beach but walked straight into a very large fist. He was floored onto his ass and spat blood between his legs. Then his military training kicked in and he attempted to jump back up, but the barrel of a gun was placed squarely in his face. Its owner smiled and motioned to him with the pistol.

"No trouble, you get into car"

He wiped the blood from his mouth and spat again

"Okay, Okay"

He slowly rose from the floor then span round using his weight to take the gun from his assailant, bloody hell these blokes were tough. He managed to twist it from him and started to raise the weapon when the whole world suddenly went dark.

The last days of the Empire - 1954

He was first introduced to his future wife by a friend at a party at the Royal Police Officer's Mess in Kula Lumpur. It was spring and he was now working as an officer for the fledgling CID, although still run by the British and staffed mostly by English officers. Her name was Mary, and she was a nurse working out of KL Hospital. He noticed her from the moment he walked into the room. She was only a shade above five foot two but in a land of petite women the moderately sized are crowned Queen. He thought at first that she was British; her features were definitely Western. He even questioned for a fleeting moment that she could possibly be Spanish; her hair was jet black and her eyes the colour of honey. Her hair was curled at the sides and kept up with hairclips, as was the style. Her dress an immaculate flowing white and cream creation that reached midway between the ankle and the knee. He heard her laugh and knew he was smitten; properly so.

He only later found out she was a foundling left on the steps of The Church of the Assumption in Goerge Town - Father Michael had named her Mary in honour of both Jesus' Mother and Mary Magdalene; for which he imagined was the source of her conception. Eurasian children in the Father's experience, outside marriage, mostly sprang from the dance halls and massage parlours frequented by British and Irish soldiers and staffed by local women; Malay and Chinese. There were numerous occasions when he'd found a 'babe in arms' wrapped in a sarong mewling on the church's front steps. In its good grace the Church had accepted them all into the fold and the orphanage. Here under the guiding hands of the sisters she'd excelled in her studies and was now a successful nurse. She was the youngest nurse to ever be promoted to the rank of sister at Kuala Lumpur Hospital. She loved her job and the people she worked with.

Her background meant nothing to him; after all wasn't he also the orphan with no country, no legacy nothing to go back too and hence nothing to lose. As a nurse who was working during the insurgency she'd already had plenty of experience of the damage done by bombs and guns. She understood what he'd been through and the mental scars such actions leave.

The dream took him from KL to remote villages on the coast to the north of the country. He remembered picnics of delicious spicy fish and rice wrapped up in banana leaves and washed down with coca cola or if he'd remembered to bring the flask hot Teh Tarik - poured tea, condensed milk with mountains of sugar.

He remembered how they made love in his car, on beaches, in small hotels in far-away forgotten towns and in grand hotels in the capital. He remembered her beautiful face and her laughter. She was also very witty and funny; something he'd never found in a woman before, and he felt that was worth its weight in gold.

Green Vipers, Dark Days - a lifetime in the past

They'd honeymooned for three nights at the beautiful Bellevue Hotel; with one of the greatest views in SE Asia. It sits upon Bukit Bendera (Flag Hill) at the very top the island of Penang or Pulau Penang (the Pearl of the Orient). Sandwiched in-between Sumatra to the west and peninsular Malaya to the east. More than six thousand miles away from London and almost three thousand feet above sea-level it's where the Imperial British escaped to every summer to avoid the malaria carrying mosquito.

The view from the top of the hotel allows you to see straight across the straits to the jungles of the mainland. From the gardens the views are breath taking; small colonial houses shrouded in mist a-top foothills, you look out across the island's capital, George Town, with its Mosques, Hindu temples and bleached white colonial government offices. Further still is the blue azure of the Indian ocean; always warm and mostly welcoming.

Every night they would catch the last funicular train up the hill from the town and eat late in the Hotel restaurant. They'd make love into the early hours and sleep soundly: free from all the turmoil and death back on the mainland. Every morning, they rose after ten and took breakfast above the gardens on the wooden terrace. Here above their heads was a thick green roof of vines, which provided protection from the sun and occasional monsoon rains, but it wasn't the vines that were fascinating but what they harboured.

The owner of the hotel a certain Mr Halliburton was obsessed with the enticer of Eve - the snake. He had several of the beasts in glass cages around the hotel but had reserved the vines above the veranda for his favourites, the Green Philippine Pit Viper. His ophiophilism extended to feeding them the occasional dead mouse, and they certainly kept the rat population down.

A small sign on the wall stated,

'Please Do Not Touch - Venomous Snakes'

After a day or so you eventually got used to them, they weren't predatory or aggressive. For the most part they did not venture south onto one's breakfast but merely coiled amongst the vines, wrapped together; so one could not make out the difference between vines and snakes. It was a good analogy of life, what's good, what's bad. Why is this person trying to love me and this one trying to kill me?

He was pondering these thoughts in the darkness as he starred into what he thought was a writhing mass of vipers and vines in the ceiling above his head. As he came around, he realised it was a mass of rotting electrical wiring that was exposed in the collapsed roof of an old building. He tasted blood in his mouth and realised that he was no longer on a colonial hill in SE Asia twenty years ago.

Nebraska Ave, Santa Monica - 1971

His head was pounding, and he felt woozy. He coughed and moved his head forward trying to get up. He realised he was strapped to an old chair and peering through the darkness, some sort of old warehouse or factory. He heard movement behind him. Then a flash of light from the corner, a cigarette was lit, and smoke exhaled. A large shape moved forward into the brightness provided by two old sky lights in the ceiling; the room looked like the interior of an old warehouse. The wooden floor rasped as the suited brute dragged a chair behind him dumped in unceremoniously a few feet away and slumped into it.

The man was aged in his early fifties in a fashionable black suit. He was large about two hundred and fifty pounds, muscle running to fat, and around six feet tall. He looked ex-army, like he knew how to handle himself, and his face had more than a few scars. He smiled at him, as he smoked a thin cigarette and smoothed the thinning blonde, grey hair across his scalp - not that he cared about the thinning of the hair the action merely soothed. He could hear two others in the room, they stood either side of him, he thought *if they wanted me dead, I'd be dead already - which is good news.*

He smiled at his captive,

"So, been out of Mother Russia for long?"

The man burst out with laughter was clapped his hands together. The laughter continued for a while then he sighed and lit another very thin cigarette. He offered one but the Spaniard declined.

"Very good, very good my friend. I can tell you are ex-forces, maybe ex-special forces. You are like me you recognise your own. But no I am no Russian, I am better - I am Ukrainian. A loyal member of the Communist party since 1936. *Polkovnik* or err how you say Colonel since '59."

"Well excuse me if I don't stand and salute, I'm a little tied up right now."

As if the emphasise this he struggled in his bonds. The man laughed again.

"Ha, Ha. You, you have funny English humour"

He then dropped his smile,

"Or should that be Spanish. You see we know who you are my friend, we know why you are here and well, we want you to stop."

The Colonel offered another cigarette, again it was refused. The Colonel stood up and began to pace, he held his cigarette upright in his hand as if it were a torch, like Marshall Tito.

"What do you know of luck?"

He stopped and took a hit of smoke then continued to pace.

"I know much of this luck. Two years ago, in Kiev my wife fucks my brother. I catch them in the horrible act and am deviated, no, no devastated.
Yes, that's better. My brother feels remorse and, as he is senior member of Politburo in the country, he gets me new posting. I am no longer assistant minister for regional trade in Ukraine but Cultural Attaché to Russian consulate in Los Angeles. Now I have sunshine, many girls, I

travel to the Las Vegas I gamble, I eat your rich American food, I take long walks on beach and live the good life. My brother is stuck in Kiev with my old fat wife, no sunshine no girls no Vegas. Now you tell me who is lucky? Who is it?"

"You've got a good tailor too!"

The Colonel stopped and smiled.

"Thank you. Yes, he's a Jew and he does excellent work" he continued,

"Now where was I? Oh yes, I tell you Spaniard it is I who is lucky, not him, not him. And now you are lucky, very lucky because I will save you from this. I am your, how is it said, your benefactor."

The Colonel smiled at him and the Spaniard shook his head

"Yes, I really feel under the protection of a benefactor tied to a chair in this shit hole Colonel."

"I'm sorry my men, they are too heavy handed. I apologize."

"*Razvyazat yego*!"

He gestured to the two men at the back of the room. They were the two who'd bundled him into the car. One untied him and the other handed him an open bottle of coke, which he drank thirstily. He fumbled in the pockets of his jacket and pulled out a stub of a cigar which one of the two heavies lit for him. Exhaling a plume of blue grey smoke into the dimly lit room he slicked back his hair, leaned forward and looked directly at the Colonel.

"What exactly do you want? And please be fucking specific comrade."

"Please call me Dmitry."

"OK Dmitry. Why are we having this conversation?"

"OK I'll be direct. You are here to do job? Yes?"

"Maybe."

The Russian rose and, once again, began to pace, his arms folded behind his back. He turned towards him

"Hmmm Maybe. OK Maybe or might. But we know you are here to do a task, a task who the Americans dare not touch. We'd like you not do this please. Just leave the city, go back to London. Enjoy living in your free western democracy. No one would blame you for just going home. It's been a trying time for you."

He smiled at the Russian, then shook his head,

"Colonel I can neither confirm nor deny I am here working on behalf of anyone. I am merely a private citizen in Los Angeles seeking new business opportunities."

"And now those business opportunities have come to an end, and you must return home."

"And why would I want to do that Colonel, sorry Dmitry?"

"Because it could end in your death."

Santa Monica Beach - Morning

The Russians dumped him on the sidewalk, a stone's throw from the hotel. He'd guessed they didn't want to be seen if his hotel was being monitored by the Feds or the Agency. He had no idea it was being shadowed by either, but they obviously wanted to be safe rather than sorry. Before he'd left the rundown warehouse, he'd quizzed them some more about why they wanted him to cease all activities in LA, obviously he'd not given the game away. Dmitry had mentioned politics and global peace and strategic alliances. All of which didn't seem to match the target he'd been given; domestic, organised crime, clean slate needed on the West Coast etc. He pondered these thoughts as he entered his hotel lobby, grabbed the keys from the front desk and headed upstairs. It was just after 10am and he didn't notice the dark green sedan that had followed him along Ocean Avenue.

He was met with a broad smile as he entered his room,

"Well hello stranger, glad to see you again."

The hulking form of Jack Bradley was sat in the lone comfy chair by the window, still dressed in his powder blue suit and a straw trilby hat.

"I wish I could say the same. Looks like security here is as tight as ever."

Bradley rose from the seat

"Now don't worry about that my friend, you can't blame the management. I have the skills to break into almost anywhere. After the war I was the main guy in Berlin to see about securing secrets from behind locked doors, for both the OSS then the CIA."

"So, burglary is a big skill set for spies?"

"Well let's just say I was more of a private entrepreneur before I got caught. Then it was either the stockade or work for the government. Not much of a choice for an army corporal."

"I imagine not."

"But like I say everything is OK. The weapon is still hidden behind the wardrobe. We've also been given the green light for go on Tuesday. Hey, what happened to your mouth; you get into a fight?"

"Women problems."

Bradley laughed, they both laughed. He walked past the G-Man and opened the large wooden window letting in ozone and sunlight. He then sat and starred directly at Bradley. He decided to keep his chat with his new friends from the USSR secret; that's a card he felt he may need to play later.

"Alright, I need full disclosure. Tell me again everything you know and don't leave anything out."

Bradley took a deep breath and looked out across the bay, reflecting the Californian sunshine off the perfect blue Pacific.

"Alright but not here. Let's grab some brunch at the diner on the corner. I'd prefer to do this somewhere where I know now one's listening."

Diner, Santa Monica Beach, Sunday Moring

"Who is Paul Dragna again?"

Jack Bradley didn't respond he just handed over a plain brown file marked 'FBI' and 'Classified Investigation File' and began to tuck into, what looked like, the biggest breakfast in California. There was ham, eggs, hash browns, tomatoes, pancakes, sausages and steak; enough to feed the state. Bradley spoke hurriedly between mouthfuls.

"He's the heir to the Dragna crime syndicate in Los Angeles, California, hell the whole West Coast. His father effectively ran the mob here for decades."

Another huge mountain of eggs, ham etc were wolfed down.

"Nothing happens on the West Coast without his say so. He masquerades as a bar and nightclub owner but we know he's heavily involved in drug importation from Mexico, heroin from Asia and, of course, the usual racketeering and prostitution."

More food consumed, this time fried potatoes and sausage. Not a pleasant sight. Since he'd been knocked out by the goons form the USSR, he'd felt slightly sick. Bradley's gargantuan consumption of *the breakfast of champions* wasn't helping. He was sticking to black coffee and orange juice. Bradley took a break and exhaled, wiping his forehead.

"We'd like him…"

Bradley paused and looked furtively around. Then in a lower tone,

"…off the grid so to speak - ASAP."

They were sat in a train car diner overlooking the bay. They could've been anywhere in 'train car diner USA', New York, Miami, Des Moines. Even the restaurant didn't have a name, just a generic 'Diner' sign on the roof. The only reason you knew it was California was the view. The Spaniard closed the confidential FBI file and turned to look at the vista.

"Something doesn't add up. There's something you're not telling me."

"Erm I'm not sure what you mean?"

Bradley looked disconcerted. Did he know about the Russians? Why the hell were they concerned about a West Coast mobster?

"Nope it doesn't make sense. You're the FBI farming out a contract to a private British security firm. There's something else. Something more, more political."

Bradley leaned back from the debris of his massive breakfast and sighed.

"Alright, alright, we think Dragna's backing revolutionary groups in Latin and South America. He's doing drug deals with organisations, that are being backed or are at least sympathetic to left wing revolutions south of the border. In Columbia it's the FARC, the Araguaia Guerrillas in Brazil, the Party of the Poor in Mexico and in Nicaragua the Sandinista Liberation Front."

Nicaragua: he thought of Maylin and the 'revolutionary' friend she shares the house with.

Bradley took a swing of creamy coffee with, of course, a veritable sugar loaf mountain. He continued,

"Weed, heroin and the latest craze cocaine are all being trafficked over the Mexican border or flown directly from South America to California or the Southern states. From there Dragna and the mob distribute across the country. This is, of course, of concern to us at the FBI, to my superiors. But the bigger picture is that the money from these sales is indirectly funding revolution south of the border. This goes against the current national policy and folks from the CIA, NSA and a whole a lot of acronyms you never heard of are pissed. The last thing they want is another Vietnam in Latin America or, God forbid, another Cuba!"

Bradley ran out of steam and slumped back into the red leather booth they were both sharing.

"So, what you're saying Mr Bradley is that this isn't just a local crime figure we're targeting but someone who's really pissed Uncle Sam off big time?"

"In a word, yes. Our contract with you and Lodestar is to eliminate him on behalf of us and a heck of a lot more folk higher up the food chain."

"Bugger me. I wish I'd asked for more money. About that, when will the final payment be made?"

"The day of the job. As requested, a numbered Swiss bank account. Just as before."

He looked at Bradley still not convinced he was hearing the whole story but in this game he'd spent years being treated like a mushroom; kept in the dark and fed shit. He smiled and re-lit an extinguished cigar stub.

"Then Mr Bradley as our business is to be concluded on Tuesday and as today is Sunday. I'm taking the rest of the day off."

"We'll be in touch tomorrow to let you know when and where."

"Until then Mr Bradley; now I must go and enjoy some of this California lifestyle I've been hearing so much about."

Pacific Coast Highway - early 1971

It was like a scene from a movie he'd never seen, a dream he'd never had and an unfulfilled desire he never realised he had harboured. But driving a Mach 1 Ford Supra Cobra Mustang with almost three hundred horsepower along Pacific Coast Highway north towards Monterey Bay with a beautiful woman in the passenger seat was one of the most satisfying experiences in his forty years on the planet.

The car itself sounded like nothing he'd even heard, more like a mythical beast than a machine. Forest green with a black racing stripe and tan leather interior; it looked as good as it drove. Which was insane; zero to sixty in under eight. Cars like this simply did not exist on the other side of the pond. If you were lucky, you owned an MG, which was almost twice as slow. More amazing than this, he'd hired it from a car rental place just off Sunset. He'd merely had to show some ID, part with some cash and he was cruising along in a beautiful lethal weapon on the sunny streets of LA.

He'd entered the car rental office with the intention of getting a standard car to see the sites and scout out a couple of good locations to run to should the proverbial hit the fan. It was a modern corporate establishment, one of probably fifty across the state, red and white logo with lots of keen young salesmen rushing around in ties and short sleeve shirts trying to help you as much as they could. He found it somewhat disconcerting. In Britain people did everything they could to dissuade you from buying their product or service. Staff were rude, no one offered help or advice. There was always some retired World War Two Officer in charge whose main *raison d'etre* seemed to be to convince you that you were not the 'right sort' and this product or service shouldn't be offered to your kind i.e. a class below him. That's if you could even find a company who rented cars.

Here in the states nothing could be further from the truth; they were literally talking you in to the best deal, they couldn't be more helpful and kept asking 'Sir may I help you'. He did note that they were a little rude until they found out he was from England. Slowly he'd realised that looking Spanish in California wasn't always the best way to make friends and influence people. But when he opened his mouth and his British Officer Received Pronunciation rolled out; they behaved as if her Majesty herself was about to rent this stupidly powerful muscle car.

"Might one enquire the cost of leasing one of your more exclusive vehicles?"

"Of course, Sir. For a mere a hundred dollars down you can lease this car for … say are you from England"

He looked at the Californian, who was pimpled and no more than twenty-five.

"Why yes how perceptive of you to notice dear boy. Now where's the most powerful car in your lot?"

Half-an-hour after entering the car rental building, he was back out on the hot blacktop in a beast of a muscle car smoking a cigar and listening to jazz on the radio from a station in Monterey. He decided today would, as the Lord had ordered it, be a day of rest. Time to visit his favourite Nicaraguan and head up the coast following the sound of Miles Davis to its source. He put any thoughts of the work ahead far to the back of his mind.

Maylin had eagerly agreed to accompany him north to investigate Big Sur, Carmel and Monterey. Although she had lived in LA for almost two years between her studies and work, she'd barely seen the city let alone the state. She'd packed a small picnic of Cokes, boiled eggs, bread, cheese and fruit. She placed it carefully into the back and fastened her seatbelt as they sped off. She looked amazing tight blue jeans with, if it were even possible, a tighter gingham shirt. She looked very attractive, with a book smart's edge.

"Hey great car."

He smiled

"You like it?"

"Es muy hermosa."

"Wow you like it that much. Had I known you were impressed by Detroit steel I'd have rented it earlier."

She looked around the interior and stroked the dash.'

"This is one amazing car. And they let you hire it?"

"My character is clean without a stain thank you madam."

She smiled,

"I'm sure it is but this is one big expensive car to be hiring out. Back in Managua you'd be lucky to hire some old Studebaker or even a motorbike. Mostly people just hire a driver."

"London's the same. Most people who don't own a car just take the bus."

The car took a sharp right and sped onto PCH - Pacific Coast Highway - a long coastal road that stretches from north of San Francisco all the way south past Los Angeles towards San Diego and the border with Mexico. They were headed north towards Monterey Bay with the sea on their left and the wind in their hair. She cracked open a Coke for them to share. He took a small sip handing it back to her

"So what are you studying for?"

She laughed and almost choked on the bottle as she took another swig.

"What am I studying or why am I studying?"

He smiled and put up his hand in supplication.

"Sorry I meant, what are you reading at university. Not why are you there."

"I'm currently doing a masters degree in politics at UCLA. Good college; not sure about the course."

"Hey, I think politics a growth industry these days. Look, five hundred years ago you had one king, one ruler. Now with all this democracy and threats to democracy; there's more than enough jobs to go round. Politics is an industry that seems to have turned itself into a pretty huge corporation."

"Cynical, very cynical: but true. No, I mean I'm not sure I know what to do with the paper after I qualify. I could go back to law in Nicaragua, work for a candidate or an elected official. My problem is I've started to like the states. It's a free country with opportunities. I also like the people here; you can say what you want without fear of reprisals."

"You like the people here? Present company included?"

"Of course, present company include."

He smiled and put on his Persol sunglasses, speeding towards the symbolic home of jazz on the West Coast. Maybe it was the company, maybe his relaxed state of mind or just the jetlag but he failed to notice the black Chevy tailing them.

China Cove, Point Lobos, Pacific Coast Highway

She was staring deeply into his eyes; post coital bliss flowed over them, making them both dizzy. He held her gently in his arms on a large tartan blanket that had been their dining table and was then briefly their bed. She picked a blade of dried grass from his hair and smoothed his locks behind his ear. His hair was far longer than it had ever been before, and he was wearing some very un-Officer Club attire, linen slacks and a silk shirt. Maybe California was rubbing off on him. She kissed him again.

"That was good, very good. I can tell you've done this before. How old are you?"

He smiled,

"What a question. A gentleman, Maylin, could take offence at that."

"What we just did wasn't the act of a gentleman."

He laughed,

"You're right. OK well let's just say I remember World War Two, but I was too young to fight in it."

"Hmmm over thirty then but under forty?"

"Erm yes something like that. Now I could ask you the same question but I'm guessing you're the good side of thirty."

"A lady never reveals her age *Señor*."

She smiled and wriggled out from his embrace and stood up gazing out across the bay. She lit a cigarette, inhaled deeply and blew smoke across the horizon. The view, which they had to themselves, of China Cove was stunning; evergreen trees dotted the white cliffs which ran down to a green blue bay of Pacific. It'd been home to Chinese immigrants in the 1850s who'd sailed across the Pacific to get rich in the California Gold rush. After a few years many had changed back to their former employment of fishing instead and the whole area up to Monterey was party to that industry. But now the land and beaches had been turned back to nature as part of a national park and apart from the footpaths you'd have thought this place had been free from human existence for a thousand years.

They'd parked the Mustang in a deserted little lot just off PCH and decided to trek towards the coastline. China Cove sounded like an exciting location, and they were not wrong. After eating lunch they'd decided that the only possible course of action was to honour the beauty of the place in an ancient form of human coupling. Plus, as they both agreed following the act, they were horny.

Maylin took another drag from her cigarette and looked out across the Pacific towards Asia.

"Too cold to swim today I think?"

He nodded in agreement,

"Yes, I tried back in Santa Monica Bay; it was as cold as the Atlantic. Do you still want to try and get up to Monterey?"

"It's almost four, let's get back. I have to work tomorrow and they'll be other days."

He liked the sound of that 'other days' it inferred a slightly more long-term relationship than he was used to. He brushed the sand and grass off his trousers and shirt and joined her looking out across the cove.

After a while they packed up the remains of their picnic in a canvas bag and started back towards the car. The trail was dusty and dry, a mixture of rocks and sand gave way to scrub bush wither side of the path. After fifteen minutes of relatively hard hiking, they were back at the car. But they were not alone.

Parked behind their monster rental was a large black Chevy sedan and stood either side of it were two very large looking Russians.

Department of State - Internal Document

Do Not Copy

Transcription (Redacted) of recorded phone call between Subject A and Subject B by the Central Intelligence Agency.

Time (Start): 15:41:01 (Pacific Standard Time)

Date: Sunday 02/07/71

Audio - Phone call ringing

Subjects A ██████ ████████ & B ████████ ████████

B - Hello, Chelsea 41██

A - Hello Mr Fraser and how are we today?

B - Bloody hell Bradley what do you want. Do you know it's almost eleven at night and you're calling me at home on a Sunday? This better be good.

A - Yep, it's good, all is fine. I'm just calling to confirm we are green lit for go on Tuesday. Your payment will clear then and ████████████████

B - What? Yes of course (subject pauses and coughs). Is this line secure? It better be otherwise I do not know you and you can bugger off right now.

A - Fraser I am on a secure line, this is a scrambled line, I work for Director ████████. Everything is fine.

B - Alright. Good. I'm glad to hear it. Now just to confirm when the job goes ahead, we will receive funds into the pre-arranged Swiss account.

A - Yes, that is correct.

B - And there will be no way to connect Lodestar to this event in any shape or form.

A - No way at all. He is a lone gunman, with a Spanish background; who's now a hired gun a mercenary for a left-wing group who want this man dead. It'll be seen as house cleaning by the South American left, in particular ██████████████████, getting rid of a man who's no longer useful. We'll leave documents and money on the body that'll infer that.

B - Hmm (breathing) I'll be sad to see him go, he's been a great asset to the firm. You're aware he's very resourceful.

A - We'd expect no less but unless he's accompanied by a battalion of Marines your man is going down.

B - Bradley he's ex-special forces; he's very capable.

A - He's toast buddy. Once the job's done, so is he.

B - Well good luck and we look forward to payment *(noises, voices heard off the line)*. I'm coming darling. I've got to go Bradley. Goodbye.

Line is cut leaving dial tone.

A - Goodbye you Limey fuck.

China Cove, Point Lobos, Pacific Coast Highway

There's always a specific time in life when something occurs that changes everything. It could be a big thing, someone wins the lottery, someone is killed in a bus crash. Alternatively, it could be a minor one, leaving late for the bus means you missed out on the bus crash, or getting somewhere early meant you got on the bus crash and are now feeding through a tube. It could be nothing to do with you at all but some sort of butterfly effect. A wave in the south Pacific hits a rock at a certain angle with causes a boat to swerve to the left rather than the right, some of the fish that are caught fall overboard leaving one particular fish on top of the pile. That fish is sold at a market in Okinawa to a famous Sushi chef who serves it to the Japanese foreign minister, at a special banquet, but it makes him ill, and he cannot attend an international nuclear negotiation in Seoul. And before you know it's World War Three.

This event was on the smaller side but made some life changing events happen. Russians in black suits armed with handguns tend to do that.

"You need to fly back to London."

They were the same men he'd encountered yesterday: Dmitry's men. The larger of the two, which was like saying the larger of the Rocky Mountains as opposed to the second largest, stepped forward towards them. They looked almost identical, one blonde one dark haired, both looking like Slavic giants who'd come directly from the Steppe.

He met the man’s gaze and stepped in front of Maylin protectively.

“No, I suggest you both fuck off!”

The parking area was deserted apart from the two Soviets and themselves. The men stood in front of the large black Chevy; one talking and the other, the smaller man, defiantly smiling.

“You, woman come with me, I’ll drive you back to LA. And you Spanish can go with Antov; you’ll collect your passport and head out to airport.”

“And if we say no?”

The blonde Russian smiled and started to reach under his arm. But he was too slow, and his grin dropped when he realised he was facing a small black Walther PP pistol. Small, only a .32, but it’d kill you at this range. It was an extra ‘emergency’ gun he’d picked up from the dealer in South Central. No serial number, that’d been filed off, no history, not legal in any sense of the word. A Saturday Night Special, albeit a very nice one.

“Now both of you throw your guns over here” the Spaniard waved the Walther “slowly and raise your hands in the air once you’ve done it.”

The two soviets complied. They tossed their weapons at his feet and reached for the sky. The Spaniard pointed towards the dirt.

“Now, get onto the floor and place your hand behind your heads.”

They both lay down in the dust, covering their suits in California dirt.

He turned and winked at Maylin who stared at him shocked and slightly open mouthed. He walked around the side of the car, took out a small switch blade and stabbed viciously into the two rear tires. He walked back to the larger of the Soviets lying on the floor. He pulled back the man's head, grabbing his blonde hair and put the pistol into his cheek.

"Now tell that Ukrainian cunt you work for that I am here to stay and if he sends you two fucking arseholes like you idiots after me again, I'm going to end his life."

The Soviet's eyes widened and he nodded in acknowledgement. The gun suddenly went off, it wasn't aimed at the prone man's head but the near front tyre of the Chevy. It burst and hissed with escaping air and the Spaniard turned towards Maylin, placing the pistol in the waistband of his trousers.

"Let's go."

She stared back at him unable to move. She'd seen a lot of weird and strange events in Nicaragua but nothing like this. Who the hell is this guy?

"Maylin. Let's go,"

He touched her arm gently but with intent,

"Maylin, now."

They got into the Mustang and roared up the hill towards PCH in a cloud of dust.

Pacific Coast Highway, California, early 1970s.

The journey back to LA was quieter than the journey out. The late afternoon wind whistled into the car from the Pacific. It accompanied the rumbling of rubber on tarmac as they motored along. The road carefully following the contours of the hills and always giving the driver panoramic views of the coast. The wind and the sound of the road where the only things that you could hear because the two occupants were not talking. She had her legs curled up underneath her in the passenger seat and was smoking cigarette after cigarette. He meanwhile was hiding behind dark sunglasses staring out across the highway. It was a long journey back to Los Angeles.

After the incident when they'd both jumped into the car and motored back onto PCH he'd tried to clear the air.

"Maylin look, let me explain"

"Explain, explain what; who are you?"

"Look it's just a business deal that's gone a little off track. We've had some communication problems…"

She pulled off her sunglasses and starred at him, one of those hard 'do not bullshit this Latina' stares.

"Communication? Communication? The man was going to pull a gun on you cabron? A gun is more than just a communication issue. Mierda just tell me this isn't anything to do with el drogas!"

He laughed, not a great move, she swore again in Spanish and looked as if she were about to go for him, full on Latin meltdown. Her face was flushed, and the green eyes danced with fire.

"Hey, hey calm down it's not drugs, it's not like that, well it's not illegal. Look I'm working for the government. I can't tell you more than that its, its complicated."

She said one phrase to him and turned away from him to stare at the hills, arms folded. She said the same phrase again after a lengthy fifty-minute silent drive back to her apartment in Venice Beach. This time the phrase was not directed to him but he heard it as she slammed the door shut on the car and stormed up the path towards her small two bedroom house.

"Hijo de puta."

And she was right he was a son-of-a-bitch.

Sunset Blvd, Pacific Palisades, Sunday Afternoon.

He'd dropped the car off at the depot on Pampas Ricas; they were well into the suburbs of Los Angeles, north of Santa Monica. The nice clean men at the car rental offices couldn't have been more helpful. As he'd only taken it for a day they'd said he could keep it until tomorrow; the car had lost its appeal after the incident up the coast, and he knew the Soviets would be hunting for it and him. He thanked them kindly, apologizing for the dust on the car, and tipped the nice clean man a couple of dollars. He told him he was amazed they were open on a Sunday. The man retorted,

"But Sir we're open every day of the year; why wouldn't we be?"

He smiled and thanked the man again; the Americans had no real concept that the rest of the world operated from 9 to 5 Monday to Friday (if you were lucky) and were closed for at least an hour every lunchtime; make that two-three hours the nearer you got to the Mediterranean. He thought - with that sort of work ethic the Americans would be in charge of the planet within twenty years. The nice clean man in the short-sleeved shirt called out towards him as he strolled off.

"Sir, can we call you a cab?"

"Call me anything you want I'm off to walk along the beach."

Again, a peculiar habit of the British to desire to walk to clear one's head. He may have been born in Spain, but the British Empire had worn off on him. Moments later, as he was trying to cross Sunset, a huge dark green Ford flashed his lights and honked its horn. It pulled over to the curb side beside him; he instinctively jumped back thinking that it could be the Russians. A friendly Latino face popped out of the window and smiled.

"Hey Senor - you need a ride hombre?"

It was Jesus from Walnut Cabs, gold tooth, and matching sunglasses glittering in the dying rays of the day. He walked over to the car, leaning on the roof with his arm.

"Hola Jesus, que tal?"

"Bien, muy bien gracias Señor. Y tu?"

"Un poco casando. Very tired, now I don't suppose you know where I could get a drink?"

"Hey Jesus knows everything - el mundo."

He jumped into the back of the cab.

"Then let's go yo compadre."

The dark green monster of a car pulled out sharply and sped off towards PCH. They then took a left onto Wiltshire Boulevard and headed away from the ocean. The area looked rougher, more rubbish, less white faces. He thought, this must be where the people live who work for those with the sea views. Although it was nothing like the inner-city decay he'd seen in South Central. They passed Douglas Park and a sign for Mid-City; the radio was blaring Salsa Hits from a station called 'Boss Radio' it was apparently '*Numero Uno*' or so the station ident kept telling the listener between songs. The car peeled off right and then second left down a small street, which looked more like an alleyway. He turned to Jesus,

"This isn't where I get rolled?"

"Que? Rolled oh" Laughing "No, no robado, this is where I drink."

Cantina Cerveza, Los Angeles.

It was a dick hang, plain and simple, a working-class bar with just a bunch of dudes hanging out. Unlike the traditional pubs of Britain, bars in the States weren't friendly places of banter, serving hot food and wise rhetoric from a sage old landlord; the place decorated with horse brasses and weird unknown agricultural implements from years gone by. But then he reminded himself that most boozers in London were rough and tumble establishments on the edges of criminality which made the rash decision to serve unhinged people, mostly men, copious amounts of alcohol. The only difference in LA was that there were no licensing laws, and one could drink all day and all night. Which made America the land of free and definitely the home of the brave.

Jesus escorted him inside, there were no windows just illuminated signs behind the bar and above the pool tables. More Latino music emanated from the jukebox, this time it was some sort of rock band, playing Latin beats but singing in English. There was the click and clack of the pool tables and the low rumble of chattering male voices; the place was moderately packed for a Sunday night. They made their way through the smoke fug and grabbed a booth towards the back. Ideal he thought for an exit in a hurry.

'Yeah, I know it's pretty rough in here Mijo, but the crowd are OK; there's no trouble. Just hombres trying to get a little drunk before they get back to the construction site tomorrow. Plus, it's near my house.'

He smiled and ordered a beer from a passing waitress.

'You want the same Ingles?'

'Si'

They sat in silence and smoked until the drinks arrived, courtesy of a very small mestizo waitress, no more than five-foot; you could see the Indian and Spanish blood. She smiled sweetly and served the drinks. Jesus picked up the tab

"Gracias Jesus."

"De nada."

"So how you like LA so far?"

"It's all right. To be honest I'm here for work and as soon as that's finished, I guess I'm heading back to London."

"Si, England. It's a green and pleasant land no?"

Strange thing for a Mexican taxi driver to say, maybe he'd heard it in an old British movie.

"It's OK, the people are reserved and it's a little too uptight but it's mostly peaceful and when it's not raining the place is, si bien, muy bueno."

The men sat in silence and Jesus took a handful of the peanuts the waitress had left while he lit a small cheroot cigar. He rolled the smoke in his mouth and breathed out though his nostrils. The nicotine calmed him.

"Your business here Señor, can I ask what it is?"

He looked across the table into Jesus' eyes; was this man searching for something?

"You can ask, but I cannot tell you. It's confidential."

Jesus took a sip of beer, and looked up, intent in his eyes.

"Si confidential, I get it. Well, if you need any help Mijo, as you are Spanish, then Jesus is always willing to help. Anything Señor, anything."

Before he could respond Jesus rose suddenly from the table.

"I gotta get home, can I drop you back at your hotel?"

He looked quizzically at the taxi driver. He figured the man was trying to make a little extra cash, whatever the business was he was involved in. Might be a handy person to know if he needed to get rid of a body.

"Thank you, Jesus, I'm going to stay for another few beers. I'll let you know if I need any help. I have your card."

The two men shook hands.

"Anything tio, and I mean anything."

Then Jesus left waving goodbye to the staff behind the bar. He ordered another beer then headed off to the toilet. On the way back to his booth he signalled to the waitress for another beer and picked up a rumpled copy of La Opinion, lying on an empty table. It was Los Angeles' Spanish-language daily newspaper, and despite being Friday's copy he spent an enjoyable few minutes reading about a strange country in his native tongue: 'Drought in Los Angeles causes poor harvest', 'Latino student excels at UCLA', 'Nicaraguan Opposition Leader in LA for Pan American talks'; this last story was next to a picture of a small looking Latin man in glasses. He heard his beer being placed on the table and glanced up to thank the waitress. But this was not the face he met

"Hello Spanish, enjoying your newspaper?"

Still dressed in a sharp black suit, matching tie and white shirt was Colonel Dmitry. Christ it was Sunday, he thought, does this fucker never take a day off. He glanced round looking for the Russian Tweedledum and Tweedledee, but the two henchmen were nowhere to be seen.

"Calm down Spanish, my men have gone home it's only me. I wish just to have a calm conversation with you. You are a man of action, I can see that now, and I need to treat you with respect. So let me buy this beer and please take a drink with a fellow old soldier."

The Russian pushed the beer towards him and raised what looked like a shot of vodka, he smiled

"Salud."

He took the beer and drank as the Colonel downed the shot. He responded the toast to the Russian,

"Nostrovia."

The Russian smiled,

"Well almost for this I would say *Vashe zrodovye.* Its means *to our health* and as former military men I think it's appropriate to the situation we find ourselves in here now."

He picked up the remains of his cheroot and lit it, not noticing he was blowing smoke into the Colonel's face. The Colonel smiled and lit his own cigarette; it smelt sour compared to the cigar.

"So, Colonel, or is it Dmitry?"

The Russian smiled and shrugged

"Why do you think I'm a military man?"

The Colonel inhaled deeply and taped the ash from the end of his harsh cigarette numerous times into the ashtray; there was no ash on the end it looked like he had a nervous tic; a tell.

"Spanish, we know who you are. We know you're from Asturias; your family were killed not long after the civil war. You lived in Madrid and then somehow, we don't know how, you end up joining the British army and fighting in Malaya. First you fight as a soldier, then special forces, erm SAS. You kill many Chinese CT's, communist terrorists as you say. Then you are police for Malaysia, CID then more lately mercenary, gun for hire in Africa, Middle East, Far East and now here in US of A. You are here to kill."

"You seem to know a great deal, Colonel."

"Yes, the West is not very good keeping its secrets, secret. Many documents make their way to us from unsecure sources. You though, Major, Superintendent, Spanish, your reputation precedes you."

They sat in silence for a minute or two, both of them looked quite different from the bar's regular clientele of blue-collar workers. They'd now started to disappear, and the place was becoming quieter.

"So, Colonel, you want me to go home?"

"Please it is for not only your own good but also for the good of all our countries, Russia, Britain and Spain. Also, it is for the good of the Americans, but they don't know.'

He sighed and inhaled.

"They don't know, they are like children."

He smiled at the Russian and rose from the table

"Colonel I'm afraid I've got nothing to say. I'm not here to kill anyone. I'm ex-military with the emphasis on 'ex' and I'm here for a little business and maybe some pleasure. You've got the wrong man."

The Colonel sighed and stood up.

"I see I cannot convince you to give up this terrible task."

He switched back into British Officer mode; always showing a united front, no doubt. Inside his mind was buzzing with questions; mostly how the fuck do the Russians know about me.

"If that's all I'd better be making my way home. Goodbye Dmitry."

The Colonel let him pass and slumped back into his chair slightly deflated.

"Yes goodbye, I'll no doubt be reading about you in the papers."

This sentence fell on deaf ears as by now he was the only one left at the table.

Nationalist Spain, mid-20th Century.

The defeat of the Republican army in the north was as far as his family home had been touched by the civil war in the principality of Asturias. It was harsh country and almost as far north as you could go on the Spanish mainland; wild weather blew in from the Atlantic and the Bay of Biscay. Inland the hills were rolling green, with rocky outcrops poking out, in defiance of the rain and wind. He found out later, much later, that it was a land peopled by the Celts and like the people of Brittany to the north and much of Britain and Ireland, the Asturians had the blood of ancestors who had made life exceedingly difficult for the Roman Empire. It wasn't the Spain of Andalucía or the golden beaches of the Costas; this was hard land that bred hard people.

His family were farmers, from generations of the same. You leave school at twelve, you marry at twenty and just as the grandchildren arrive, in your forties, you die of disease and malnutrition. Your death accelerated by the hard-work, brutal work on the soil, in the frost, in the rain, failed crops, bad harvests, bad years, even worse lives. Despite this, despite the hardship, the grind, he'd had a happy childhood. His parents had both been in love, he thought he remembered this, he never went hungry, he spent many happy childhood days running around on their land, playing with other children and the animals. He felt part of the land, Asturias, this countryside his family, and then it all went away.

The murders of his parents, grandparents and siblings hadn't been part of the civil war it was a few years later than that and for a far more ignoble reason. Not that they hadn't been involved in the war. They'd fed men fighting on both sides. His father was a man of morality, a man of God; he couldn't see young men starve to death. When the Fangalists declared victory, he'd never been accused of any collaboration with the republicans. He'd kept too many nationalist officers fed with milk and bread from his land to fear any retribution. Although what it didn't offer was protection, protection from corrupt local cops who wanted more than just milk and bread.

He'd been tending the cattle in the field when he returned home in the early evening and found his family home burnt to the ground, the bodies of his father, mother and siblings all lying somewhere beneath the charred remains. His weeping neighbour told him that the local police captain and his men had raided the farm pillaging and raping as they went. The neighbour - an elderly woman in her seventies had heard gunshots and came over just as the men had set fire to the building. They'd left taking about the money they'd taken and the fun they'd had with the women.

The Spaniard had spent the next week sheltering in one of the outbuildings; weeping for his loss. He thought of ending it all, committing suicide, how could he go on. But he was an Asturian, a boy carved from the harsh baren land around him. Within seven days his anger was galvanized and his determination for vengeance set in stone.

He'd waited outside the police headquarters in the local town until they'd all returned from another evening of heavy drinking and revelry. Then armed with a can of gasoline he'd set the building on fire. From the vantage point of an upstairs window of an abandoned house he gunned down every single man who tried to leave the headquarters, whether or not they were on fire. He was as dispassionate as he was when he shot rabbits on his farm; a task he'd become adept at. Despite being thirteen years old he'd become an expert with his father's old Mosin-Nagant 1891 rifle and left a pile of bodies on the street. A sign of his future career. After that, his life in nationalist Spain was to be a far more chaotic one.

He fled to Madrid living homeless as a beggar. Eventually he became a sometime guide for tourists, a luggage handler (and sometimes luggage stealer) at the train station and, more often than not, a thief. He'd spent the first year living on the streets of the post-war capital, amongst the rubble and chaos after he fled Asturias. It was no place for a child and after that year he wasn't one anymore. He managed to get a room at the back of a dive bar near the city centre. The decrepit owner was an alcoholic and was far old to be running the place. The boy helped out with the lifting and carrying and for his sins was allowed a room and an occasional meal. It was an added bonus that the owner hated the police, so he was quite happy to hide a member of the criminal class on his premises.

For the next few years, he made ends meet on the very edge of society; not that there was much society left after the civil war. Crime was rife, women and children were starving on the street and despite the efforts and autocratic rule of Generalissimo Franco - El Jefe - the country was mired in chaos. The intellectuals, artists, the lawyers, professors, the doctors and nurses had more importantly the businessmen and their money had all fled the country during and after the war. The best and brightest minds were gone and those left in charge were inadequate to say the least. School cleaners became headmasters, humble army privates were made officers and bus conductors transport managers. It was the Peter Principle taken to the nth degree where managers rise to the level of their incompetence. Except in this case, it was way beyond their level of incompetence, a stratosphere above. Bad news for Spain as a country but good news for a petty thief and cunning street urchin such as himself.

With everyone being promoted above their talents the same could be said for the criminal class. The old pick pockets now turned over banks and jewellers; enhanced by an incompetent police force. Perfect conditions for a bright young man, such as himself, to make the most of the dire situation in which the country had found itself. He moved from begging on the streets to stealing wallets and occasionally purses. He was wiry and fast and could outrun most Guardia Civil; most of whom were too tired from fighting for Franco against the communists to bother with a pick pocket.

Another lucrative source of funds, he'd discovered, were to be found escorting newly arrived visitors to the capital from the central Atocha Railway Station safely to their hotels in the centre of the capital. He had discovered this as a valuable source of income after being asked to guide a freelance Argentine journalist from said station to his crappy hotel. He presumed that the weekly *Buenos Aries Gazatta*, or whatever rag the man worked for, were only paying a few pesetas per word. The journo's fee may have been small but his tip, for a street urchin such as himself was a king's ransom, it had afforded him two loafs of bread, a bottle of milk and half a packet of cigarettes. The latter not being essential for life but on the streets of Madrid in the 1940s they got you through a cold night.

His modus operandi was to wait patiently by the exit to the main station, careful to avoid the watchful gaze of both police and the station porters, who kicked them away like stray dogs. Once a likely client was spotted there would be a mad rush of street urchins to offer their services as a porter and guide.

Most who pushed their way through were little more than teenagers, but he had one big advantage. At fourteen he'd grown to almost five feet eleven; an almost unheard-of height back in 1940s Spain where malnutrition was rife. He put this down to Basque ancestry. His height and his trusty Taramundi knife - that had belonged to his father - meant he was usually successful when trying to secure a client.

These ranged from businessmen and lawyers to teachers and tourists, but the usual were journalists. They were fun to hang around with and sometimes he'd end up being an unofficial guide for the duration of their stay. They liked to get drunk and pick up whores, two things he himself decided were great pastimes.

It was in this capacity, as a guide to the back streets of Madrid, that he'd quickly learned other languages as to increase his customer base. A few words in French, Italian, Portuguese, and German went a long way. But it was his command of English that led to his eventual escape from the gutters of Spain.

Los Angeles, quarter of a century later.

He woke with sunlight streaming through the blinds of his hotel room giving his hangover that extra little zing. It took him a few minutes to work out what day it was, where he was and what exactly he was supposed to be doing. Yes, it as Monday, he was in his hotel in Santa Monica, he'd pissed off the local Russians and tomorrow he was supposed to kill a man for $100,000 dollars. The black Bakelite phone beside the bed rang. He let it go on until about the sixth ring when it had become unbearable and was starting to drill through his brain.

"Yes?"

"You ready?"

His head was muggy he had no idea who the hell the voice on the other end was

"Who is this?"

"It's me man. The man in the know, the man with the connections. Hey, no *habla Ingles* brother? Cause me no *habla Espanole*."

Fuck me he thought, as he rubbed the bridge of his nose and propped himself up in bed. It was that annoying PI who'd helped him buy the rifle.

"What do you want?"

"I wanna buy you breakfast, *huevos rancheros*, or whatever shit you Latinos eat in the morning. I got instructions for you and a piece of paper I think you're gonna want."

"Where are you?"

"I'm in reception, get your ass down here."

He dumped the phone's receiver onto the cradle and groaned. He glanced at his watch it was just after nine in the morning. Then to no one but an empty room he exclaimed

"Bollocks. Mierda de mierda!"

Diner, Santa Monica Beach, Monday Moring

It was like déjà vu. He was back in the same diner he'd been briefed by Bradley twenty-four hours earlier. It was new to him being a European, but it was typical Americana, lots of chrome, lots of red vinyl seats, the fry cook was wearing a little paper hat. A small jukebox on every tabletop gave you a selection of records to choose from; so you didn't have to get up from your seat.

Just deposit a nickel and you too can experience great songs from the past two decades; Elvis, Motown, the British Invasion and even today's rock hits.

None of which he'd ever heard of as he'd spent the past twenty years fighting in Asia and the Middle East. He did though recognise the bossa nova pianist Sergio Mendes and Frank Sinatra. Frank, he thought, was never the same singer after he left the Tommy Dorsey Orchestra.

The view though was still beautiful, Santa Monica Bay in the early 1970s; not too much development and perfect sun kissed blue skies.

He sat alone as the black PI returned from the bathroom.

"You get a company discount every time you eat here?"

"What the fuck you talking about?"

"This is where Jack Bradley briefed me yesterday and now, I'm here again? What for, so his underling can brief we some more?"

The PI was taken aback, he slowly removed his hat and lit a cigarette. He then slid into the seat opposite.

"Hey, calm down this is just the closest place to get breakfast near your hotel. Anyways don't get all riled up man; I'm about to give you a piece of paper that is worth much more than merely its weight in gold."

The PI threw him a file and he opened it. Inside was a single thick certificate embossed with the red Presidential seal; it was titled an 'Executive Grant of Clemency by direction of Richard M. Nixon' and signed by the Pardon Attorney. Smiling he looked up at the PI then began to read,

…a full and unconditional pardon for any past crimes committed in all territories of the United States of America…

It was dated from tomorrow - the day of the hit. He carefully placed the document back inside the manila folder and took a swig of his coffee.

"So, if I want to, I can shoot you now?"

The PI was inhaling his cigarette and the statement made him laugh and cough out smoke at the same time. He cleared his throat.

"I knew you were going to say that motherfucker. Yeah, you can shoot me, but you won't be getting the rest of your money. And, and don't forget those assholes up on Capitol Hill can rescind this document before you can re-holster your pistol. It's only good as long as they, and by they I mean the big FBI honcho Hoover, says it's good. Hey if Nixon's kicked out of office, then this ain't worth shit. But in the short term it will let you leave these shores and not be prosecuted straight after *the* event."

He leaned back in his seat and pulled a half-smoked cigar out of his jacket. He borrowed the PI's lighter and relit it blowing out the first hit of sour smoke. The second puff tasted better; more Cuban filler.

"What's your name?"

"Why?"

"I have to call you something."

"OK it's Al."

"Alfred? Albert? Alfonso? Alfredo?"

"Just Al. Limey!"

He laughed and so did the PI; they both sat there in silence; smoking, drinking coffee. Al picked up the menu and perused its contents.

"Hmm I am hungry. I think I want the blueberry pancakes. What are you gonna order? Some huevos rancheros? I don't think they serve burritos."

He laughed and shook his head in amazement.

"I'm Spanish you idiot not Mexican. I have never eaten either of those things. Besides which I've lived in Britain and the Far East for more than twenty years so I can only truly appreciate good Chinese food and terrible English."

Al raised his hands in supplication.

"OK man, well there ain't any of that in here. This here's an American diner."

"Very well then, against my better judgment I'll have whatever you're having."

The waitress obviously was blessed with a sixth sense as she suddenly appeared right beside them refilling coffees and making up the chit for two orders of blueberry pancakes. Whilst they waited Al opened a black leather folder and took out more documentation, this time not as formal as the Presidential Pardon. It was a very ordinary white envelope.

"OK this is the location and time."

The Spaniard opened the envelope. It contained a photograph and an address handwritten on a piece of paper. There were no markings, no official stamps, no FBI letter heads. It meant if he was caught, got shot or died then there was no trail back to the US government, the Feds or Lodestar back in London. Nothing to show a crime had been committed. He looked up at Al.

"It's tomorrow one o'clock?"

"Yep, it's a restaurant Downtown. You're in a room in an empty apartment opposite on the third floor. From the window you got a clear shot of the front."

"And his security?"

"Minimal - two, maybe three, soldiers. I'll pick you up just after eleven. Plenty of time to get set up."

"Do I have any company. A spotter?"

"Yes there's…"

They paused as the clairvoyant waitress came back and refilled up both their cups. The Spaniard thought he'd never tire of free refills; they were unknown back in London. They waited for the waitress to finish filling up both cups and smiled at her as she made her way back to the counter. Al continued.

"Yes, you got a spotter; some ex-marine called Harris. He was a Scout Sniper out of Camp Pendleton; a Sergeant, he was a big deal in Vietnam."

"OK great as long as he intends to remain a living legend then I've got no problems."

The Spaniard examined the picture of the target. It was a photograph of a Latin looking man in a sharp suit with dark sunglasses and a small fedora hat. On the back someone has scrawled *Dragna*.

"How old is this?"

"I dunno, recent, I think. He's a classic kinda guy, he dresses like Kennedy's still in the White House. These Guineas still think they're back in the old country."

He studied the photograph intently; he wanted a picture, a mental picture of this man. He wanted that face imprinted onto his brain; he needed to make sure that the target he focused on was the correct one. Despite this he had a feeling he'd seen this face before. The photograph rang a bell; giving him flashes of the same man in an open neck shirt but he just couldn't pinpoint it. He shook his head surmising he must have seen it in a newspaper, maybe a story about mafia crime families.

Within thirty minutes he was almost in Venice walking past what looked like the decaying dinosaur of amusement parks-gone-by. The Pacific Ocean Park jutted out into the sea as if it was making a final 1950's glory days of the-US-of-A stand against the rise of the past decade's counterculture. In reality it was just the burnt-out ghost of an old amusement park. Two surfers rode the waves in and out of the decaying old pier stumps.

He pealed of left and ducked and dived through the side streets of Venice. He didn't think the Russians, or the Feds for that matter, were tailing him but he wanted to cover his tracks. After doubling back on himself a couple of times, he retraced his steps down a side passageway and walked out in front of Maylin's record shop. There was a closed sign on the front and the shutters were pulled down. Outside rubbish; empty bottles and paper had collected around the alcove housing the front door. He checked round back for any sign of life, for which there was none. A man sweeping outside a barber shop opposite hailed him.

"Hey, hey mister."

He was short and in his late thirties with jet back hair swept back and a short moustache which looked like it belonged in another era.

"They ain't there, they takes Monday off. Try again tomorrow."

"Thank you."

He raised his hand in thanks to the barber and the Italian looking man did the same. OK, he thought, I'll head inland and check out her bungalow. He started towards the center of Venice. The sun was now reaching its zenith and he was beginning to sweat quite profusely although this was tempered by the breeze from the ocean. The heat here wasn't too humid unlike the jungles of SE Asia or Central America.

He'd only walked east across a few streets when he reached her bungalow. He climbed the stairs and knocked at the front door, no answer. He tapped the chimes hanging above the door, no answer. He then peered through the window, but the blind had been pulled down. He then twisted the door handle itself, no luck, it was locked. OK he thought maybe she or her roommate were sleeping in or having breakfast outback. He skirted down the side of the building but when he reached the rear veranda there was no sign of life. Chairs were stacked on the deck against the back of the building, an overflowing ashtray was on the stairs and an old rusty 50's fold-away table was resting on the wooden fence surrounding the deck. Again knocking on the backdoor had no effect. His only hope now was to try the handle and, to his surprise the door was open.

The smell hit him as soon as he entered the kitchen; sweet, metallic, and familiar. He'd killed enough people to know there was blood, a lot of it, in this building. He had a flash back to his work in Malaya with their special branch - CID - after the war. He'd been poached from the army by his old Commander, and they were 'helping' a newly independent Malaya keep on top of insurgents. He'd entered a cell to question a prisoner and nearly slipped over the pints of blood that decorated the floor, walls and even ceiling. The interrogator stood there smiling holding a baton covered in red and clumps of meat and hair. On the floor lay a broken witness who was no longer able to be questioned, for that matter, or breathe. Shocked he'd left the scene and reported the officer. Three months later he'd left the country.

He withdrew the Walther from the small of his back and scanned the kitchen, nothing. Then he headed into the living room and that's when he saw it, just above the lip of the couch. A woman's head, long black hair of a beautiful Spanish woman cascading from the crown and glistening with blood.

Venice Beach, Crime Scene, 1971

He didn't need to examine the body to know she was dead; he couldn't bring himself to look at her face. As a veteran he knew the large gunshot wound was fatal. Blood and brain matter decorated the couch and the floor. He stood there for what seemed like an eternity taking it all in but was probably no more than a couple of seconds. Then it kicked in; more than twenty years of military training. He scanned the entire house for any sign of habitation with his pistol raised and the safety catch off, but it was empty.

He took a towel from the kitchen and proceeded to wipe all the surfaces in the house he'd touched to get rid of fingerprints. Shit, he thought, he'd been there less than two days before, he made his way to the bedroom and wiped down door frames, tables then the sink in the bathroom and kitchen counter. Before he left, he went to the living again and, without touching a hair on her head, softly said goodbye to Maylin. He was struck with anger both at the people who'd done this and himself for dragging her into this situation. He wanted to cover her body but knew if he did, he'd leave more clues for the police.

He turned and left the room, then exited the building, again wiping door handles and frames. As he descended the steps from the deck he heard a whisper.

"Hey, hey, over-here, *Joder!*"

He whipped put the pistol again and crouched scanning from left to right.

"*Que Cabron,* over here"

He located the source of the voice, it was a female one, swearing in Spanish and coming from a bush outside the bungalow. The plant moved but it was hard to see who, or what, was calling him. He moved closer and saw a green eye, then a lock of black hair.

"What the…, Maylin is that you?"

"Yes, shut up, are they gone?"

"Jesus, I thought you were dead. What do you mean they are gone? Who's the body in the house?"

She slowly rose from behind the bush, hair dishevelled and with leaves decorating her jeans and t-shirt.

"I hate you but right now but I'm very glad to see you."

She stepped forward and embraced him tightly. He was suddenly struck by a realisation.

"It's your roommate, Josefina, isn't it."

She looked forlorn and nodded silently as tears silently streamed from the corner of her eye.

"She didn't stand a chance."

He looked around glancing into other building's windows and down across into the street.

"We need to get the hell out of here. Have you got a car?"

"No, no…"

"Shit we need to get you some where safe…"

She looked up and an idea struck her,

"Wait, wait Josefina's boyfriend's car is parked behind the house in the alley."

"OK let's go."

114

**'Are you a lucky little lady in the city of light,
Or just another lost angel, city of night
City of night' - James Douglas Morrison 1970.**

They turned off Lincoln on to Venice Boulevard and headed towards the 405; driving calmly but with haste. He had no idea where he was going to take her, but he'd had to get out of Venice and away from the murder scene. He turned down side streets and back lanes numerous times to ensure they weren't being tailed. When he was happy, they weren't he stuck to the main highway.

Two minutes earlier they'd made their way alongside the bungalow and into a back alley where Josefina's, boyfriend had left his car. Using the word car was a stretch of the imagination, it bore no relation to the Cobra Mustang he'd rented yesterday. This vehicle disproved the rule that Americans made the greatest cars in the world.

It was a rusted late fifties Nash Rambler wagon. A large, battered surfboard was in the back, which alluded to its usage. The door creaked as he opened it; sounding like the hinges hadn't been lubed since the slogan 'I Like Ike' had dropped out of usage. The inside was no better and stunk like a hippie's handbag; a blend of weed, sweat, stale beer and probably a couple of thousand heavy make-out sessions during the heady days of the 1960s.

Luckily the keys were hidden in the sun-visor and the engine started on the second turn. There as a much-used map of LA on the dash and after taking a quick glance at it he pointed the car towards a location that looked like it'd be quiet.

Blue smoke billowed from the car's tailpipe. It needed an oil change; but that wasn't big on his mind right now. They motored up Venice Boulevard towards the 405 but didn't turn onto the freeway. They headed underneath towards downtown Culver City. Houses, shops, factories whizzed by the car, as Maylin curled up beside him. He'd gone to put the radio on to distract them but, no surprise with this gem of a car, it was busted. They turned onto Duquenes Avenue and onto Jefferson until they came to the Baldwin Hills overlooking the city. He pulled the car to a stop, the brakes squealing in pain, just on the edge of a large empty car lot. Happy they hadn't been followed; he turned to her and took her hand.

"So, what happened?"

She explained that she and Josefina both had a day off and were intending to head up the coast to Will Rodgers Beach, catch a few rays and maybe even surf a little. Josefina's boyfriend was back East and had left them his car. The girls had tied one down the previous night, as Maylin was angry with him and her roommate was quite happy to have a few rums and smoke a couple of joints with her Nicaraguan compadre. So, they were both a little fragile on Monday morning. Maylin had gone outback to dump the trash when she'd seen the two men entering the house and then moments later two muffled bangs. He guessed they'd used a silencer as there'd been no calls to the police from neighbours.

Maylin suddenly grabbed him and clung tight to his shirt.

"And, and I just froze, I didn't do anything. I saw them and I just crouched behind that bush until, until you turned up. I feel awful, I did nothing to save her, to save Josefina."

"Maylin let me get this right, there were two men with guns and you crouching outback. There was nothing you could have done."

She began to quietly weep; survivor's guilt he remembered seeing it in his days as a soldier. He held her and a while later began to enquire again about the murder, for that's what it was,

"What did they look like?"

"One large black man in a sort of uniform and the other man, blonde in his late thirties, with long thin hair and a moustache. They both had gloves on and were carrying pistols."

"The black man; did he have a jump suit on like mechanics wear?"

"Yes, it was green like he was in the army, but he looked mucho gorda, too fat."

He remembered the dilapidated house in South Central, where he'd bought the rifle from, he said nothing.

She dried her eyes and looked at him long and hard.

"Is this something to do with you?"

"I'm afraid so."

She shook her head and looked out of the window.

"Can you tell me what's going on?"

He looked down into his hands, feeling guilt and shame. They'd obviously targeted Josefina thinking she was Maylin. Not the Russians, not the Mob but another group, slightly more sinister if that was possible. It was time to come clean with her, it was only fair.

"Is there somewhere you can stay where you'll be safe Maylin?"

"I don't know, maybe I gotta classmate who lives with her boyfriend up in Topanga Canyon."

"OK, you know her address?"

She nodded.

"Right let's get you there and I'll tell you the whole sordid story, or at least what I know on the way."

Avenue H, Torrance, Los Angeles.

He'd lived here for almost eight years. It'd been nearly five since he'd left the force, he'd spent almost a decade, after his service in Korea, with the LA County Sheriff's Department - trying to keep the peace. He loved this small avenue, just off the beach, if you leaned out on the front porch you could just catch a glimpse of the shimmering blue Pacific Ocean. Despite still being the only black man who owned a house on the street, and one of very few in the area, he liked this part of the world.

Al had been married but it hadn't worked out. It wasn't one of those clichéd relationships where the pressure of the job got to him and had affected his home life. He'd rarely talked about his police work, and the racism that was rife (on both sides of the thin blue line) but he certainly didn't let this affect him. This was a man who could eat stressful situations for breakfast. He'd come from a broken home in South Central and almost entered into a life of crime when military service came calling. Barely out of High School he'd fought at the Battle of Bunker Hill in the dying days of the Korean war. As his foxhole was overrun by Chinese soldiers, he'd covered himself in the dead bodies of his comrades. For at least five hours, until the US and Korean Marines rallied, he played possum. After that the volume of daily life and its stresses gets turned down, way down, to just a mere whisper.

Maybe that was why he split from Lisa, maybe, or maybe they just weren't compatible. Not that that mattered much now, he was an incredibly happy bachelor. He'd kept the house and her some cash and the car; there were no children. She moved in with her sister and later he heard she'd married a schoolteacher from Frisco and had moved up state. No animosity, no anger. If anything, he wished her well. No Al was a man who didn't hold grudges and saw life for how it truly was; messy and complicated.

That night he'd arrived home early from a meeting; his clients had requested more information on the status of the mark he oversaw. It was all stress, all bullshit, and he was feeling under pressure. After meeting his clients at LAX he'd felt in need of blowing off steam. It was still early, and he thought a cruise in the car would help. Trying to avoid rush hour he'd driven along Visa Del Mar just after Dockweiler Beach; it was a great run south. You got to appreciate the views across the bay, the swimmers and surfers were all starting to head home, and the sun was sinking slowly into the Pacific and turning everything red. He was smoking Camels and had the radio tuned to this weird jazz station out of San Diego. Well, it was weird to his ears all Bossa Nova and modern jazz but tonight it seemed to suit his mood and the drive.

By the time he hit Torrance and turned off onto Avenue H at Redondo Beach, he was happily tapping the steering wheel. He swerved crossed the road and pulled into his driveway; not noticing the beat-up station wagon parked just a few houses down. He got out of his car and took in the view of the sea and a deep breath of ozone. His neighbour Bob was watering the front garden, a balding middle-aged man with a substantial gut and a fucking awful pair of golf socks with sandals. White folks and their inability to dress, he mused to himself. He nodded, smiling, and waved. The white son-of-a-bitch had been an asshole to both him and his ex-wife until, that is, he'd found out Al was a cop and a Sergeant at that. From then on, he'd been the perfect neighbour.

Al locked the almost mint, galactic silver 1966 two-door Chevy Impala: he lived in Torrance, but this was still a nice car that hoods would want to boost. He made his way onto the porch and took another quick look at the vista that he saw every day; just inhaling a little more sea breeze. He opened the front door, again he was an ex-cop and there were numerous locks. Al dumped his briefcase by the front door, his jacket on the staircase and kicked off his loafers as he headed through the, sparsely furnished, living area and into the kitchen. Grabbing a tumbler from the dresser he opened the fridge and dumped in a handful of ice before making his way back to the living area, loosening his tie on the way. In the lounge he opened a small liquor cabinet that nestled next to his RCA Solid State record player and radio. There was another tall set of shelves to the left of the stereo that housed a myriad of records, LPs, 78s and even a few singles. Al mused about what to select from the vast collection as he poured a healthy three fingers of Maker's Mark into his glass. He left the glass on the side, and one could hear the ice tinkle as it began to melt. That set off the idea of pianos in his mind and he thought *'I've got it'*.

He thumbed through the newer part of his collection until he found it, Oscar Peterson Vol.2 Girl Talk. He'd purchased it last month and it simply was a transcendent piece of light piano jazz. Accessible to even uneducated ears, this wasn't Davis or Coltrane, you'd have to be a complete philistine not to enjoy this. He took the disc from its sleeve and gently blew non-existing dust from its surface - this was all part of the ritual. He then placed the record carefully onto the turn table, selecting the correct speed (in this case 33 rpm) and pressed play on the record player.

Al then waited in anticipation for the first opening bars of the great virtuoso. There was a gentle hiss and then music, such wonderful music as he reached for his whiskey and took a healthy swig. Oscar started to gently caress the piano keys.

"Well, I've come all the way from London the least you could do is offer me a drink."

Al span round reaching for his gun, which he suddenly realised he'd left in its shoulder holster underneath his jacket on the stair's banister. Facing him in one of the smaller leather chairs, which were arranged around the living space, was the Limey fuck he'd just handed over a Presidential Pardon to. The Brit was brandishing what looked like a small black Walther, at this range life threatening. Oscar stared to take the tune for a walk around the keyboard as was his way.

"Jesus, you son-of-a-bitch what the fuck do you want and how the hell did you find me?"

"Well Al, when you went to have a gypsy's at the diner I went through your briefcase and found your business card. Home address and office; how convenient for me."

"I went for a what, a gypsy's?"

"Yes, it's the Londoners or more precisely the Cockneys. They do love rhyming slang. Gypsy's Kiss rhymes with piss!"

"OK fine, what the fuck do you want?"

"I'll tell you what I want Al. I want to know who I'm really working for and who is trying to kill my girlfriend, if it's you, I can tell you now that you failed."

Oscar was now making full use of the piano's eighty-eight keys as he continued his solo break.

"Hey, I don't know what the fuck you're talking about man. Look I'm just a PI I do freelance work for the government, I'm not that high up on the food chain."

Al staggered back at into the record deck slightly knocking the tempo of Oscar and his trio of musicians. He advanced towards the black ex-cop, the Walther levelled into his face. Oscar seemed to respond and was now breaking into some serious chord changes, interspersed with notes at the higher end of the piano's range.

"I want to know what is going on Al and you better come up with a good explanation or you're going to find yourself pushing up daisies my friend."

He was overcome with anger, incensed that this PI was playing him. His voice had risen in pitch, his face was reddening, and his hand was tightening on the German handgun. Then he heard another sound above the music, a dull thud and that's when everything went black. Oscar meanwhile had reached a musical crescendo on the ivories.

Madrid 1947

John 'Jock' Roberts walked into his life two days before the Spaniard's sixteen birthday - although he looked like he was twenty if he was a day. He stood almost six foot tall by now and sported, so he supposed, a rather dashing moustache but it only served to make him look more like his true self; a cheap hood and a villain.

He was smoking a tabaco negro cigarette as he lent against the red walls of the city's Atocha Central Station. His eyes were closed in the heat of the late afternoon sun, which he was soaking up, and the bitter black tobacco had given him a slight nicotine high. It was almost as strong as a cigar and as such he was not inhaling the smoke; just letting it whirl around his mouth and blown out in pretty smoke rings. That's when he heard English.

"Bloody buggering thing."

A tall man, well over six-foot, dressed in tweed with a small red beard, flecked with grey, and round professorial glasses was trying to pick up the contents of his suitcase that'd emptied itself onto the cobbles as he left the railway station. This was an opportunity not to be missed the young man thought.

"Señor, err Sir let me help you."

The older man, who was in his forties, looked up and smiled at the teenager as he crouched down and began to help the man pick up the contents of his suitcase. Clothes, paper, pens, a stopwatch, and a hipflask were all scooped back into the battered brown leather case. He thought it strange that this man didn't seem to be worried by a stranger coming forward to help him. They both stood up and the tall man shook his hand.

"Thank you, lad, bloody catch is kaput. Now do you know which way to El Hotel Atlantico por favor."

The accent was strange, almost European, not English. He would later learn that Jock was British but also Scottish.

"Of course, Señor, it's no problem."

The man smiled again at him and pulled out a brown curved briar pipe from his coat pocket which he proceeded to light. Puffing on the pipe and adjusting his tweed hat.

"I'll pay you mind, el dinero'" flashing a handful of Peseta notes.

"Oh, thank you Señor"

The boy already had the suitcase under his arm.

"Por favor no 'Señor', Me nombre es Jock, Si, Jock." He said pointing at himself.

"Si Señor, sorry Jock." The boy nodded and smiled.

He guided Jock through the streets of Madrid with them both speaking a mixture of English and Spanish. Jock told him he was there to give a lecture at the university and there were several museums and churches he'd like to visit. He said he was on a sabbatical from the University of London, UCL, and that he'd need a guide for the next week or so if that was acceptable. The young man jumped at the chance and agreed readily, he could do with the cash. They agreed with a handshake outside the doors of Jock's once palatial hotel.

So, for the next week he guided the Scotsman from University to church to library and again another church. Jock would meet the young man and offer him the occasional lunch or dinner, paying him for his services as a guide every evening. H eventually told Jock that his family has been murdered during the war, he didn't expend on the details or the revenge that he took. In turn Jock explained, rather vaguely, of his role during the Second World War.

"I worked in intelligence; I made sure the right people where at the right place at the right time."

So, there they were, together two men who'd been affected by tumultuous world events both with their own secrets to hide.

The two developed a friendship over the next few weeks until a fateful night in Madrid that would change the Spaniard's life forever. Jock had left a message at the front desk of the Hotel Atlantico, in broken Spanish it read…

'Come to Taberna Ramos tonight at eight o'clock por favor gracias Jock.'

He'd spent the day sleeping back at his own flop house hotel until early evening then eaten a little stale bread he'd been saving in a draw at the bottom of his bed and drunk a small bottle of beer as he walked towards the back street bar. He'd taken his time but was still thirty minutes early, when he'd seen three figures in the dark alley alongside the bar. One of the three's voices he recognised; it was Jock, but something wasn't right here. His fledgling intuition was kicking in, leaving him tingling all over his body. It was the same the night his family had been killed back in Asturias.

He crept up the alley way keeping to the shadows, hugging the crumbling wall of the bar. The three men were arguing,

"Now boys don't you think we know what you bastards have been trying to do?" Jock growled

"You need to leave Madrid now *Du Hurensohn!"*

One of the other two men spoke; a low guttural accent, he'd later learn was German.

Suddenly one of the men facing Jock pulled a gun; the barrel glinted in the light thrown from the yellow sodium lamps in the main street. Now for some reason, again he had no idea why, maybe it was a sixth sense, but he knew he had to protect this Scotsman. It was weird he had no links to this man; he was just another foreigner that he could make some cash out of. But a voice inside his head said, *'make sure no harm comes to this man.'*

He began to creep closer unfolding his Taramundi pocketknife. Leaping out of the shadows he brought the blade down onto the hand of the German with the gun. The man screeched in pain dropping the weapon. He span round, a look of shock and anger on his face.

There was no time to think the young man from Asturias pulled out the blade and drove it into the gunman's chest. He gasped and clutched his left breast. Meanwhile Jock pulled a gun out of nowhere and shot the second man three times in the chest. It all happened in seconds, but it felt like a macabre dance that'd gone on for hours. The two men were slumped on the floor dead: dark black blood pooing around their bodies. Jock turned and grabbed him by the shoulders.

"Bloody Nazi bastards. Well done lad, well done. You saved my life. This is something I will not forget, you did well."

It would be sometime later that he discovered Jock was not a visiting history professor but a British MI6 agent. And that these two men, who lay dying at their feet in a dirty back alley in Madrid, were former SS offices living under the radar in Falangist Spain.

After that night his life would never be the same again. Within two days he had left Spain for London and a much belated secondary education. Within three years he was fighting with the British Forces in Malaya. He had a new father in Jock, a new country to call home and, courtesy of the British Embassy in Madrid and MI6 in London, a new name.

More than thirty years later - California

When he woke from his dreams of Spain in the old days, he swore he could still hear someone speaking Spanish. His eyes flickered open and the room was spinning and his vision blurred. He had a familiar taste in his mouth; bitter and metallic, yes that was blood. He felt around with his hands; he was face down on a rather attractive stone coloured carpet which he could just make out had been spoiled by his own blood. A pool of which was just by his face. He felt guilty about ruining the rug, well almost since he was the one lying face down bleeding on the floor.

"Ola mijo. Com estas?" the voice addressed him.

"He's awake get him up" and then someone else.

A strong pair of hands grasped him under his armpits and dragged him to a small leather chair. It took a while for him to come to his senses, he coughed, widened his eyes, and shook his head. Two knock outs in one week couldn't be good for his brain. As his vision came back into focus, he saw he was facing two men. One standing, one sat, one black, one maybe white; both looked familiar.

That's because they were, the black man was of course his PI handler Al, from whom he'd stolen the business card, broke into his home and perused both his record and whiskey collections. He now focused on the other man he was not white but Latino. It was the taxi driver, black hair and gold teeth.

"Fuck me, Jesús."

Jesús smiled and handed him a glass of water and a towel.

"Yes, it's blasphemy mijo but it's also my name. I'm sorry about the cut on your mouth, you clipped the coffee table as you went down. It was not my intention to hurt you just put you out of action for a while until we could get all this unpleasantness cleared up."

He noticed the taxi driver was speaking without a Spanish accent, he also noticed that the man was also wearing a sports jacket and that he looked more Brooks Brothers than El Hombre from El Barrio.

"Bloody hell my head hurts. What did you hit me with?"

"A blackjack, once again sorry."

Jesús showed him the cosh in his coat pocket and genuinely looked apologetic. Al handed him two pain killers; the Spaniard took them without even asking what they were, downing them with a swing of water.

"Is your name even Jesús?"

"Yes, it is. Jesús Juan Garcia at your service."

"And who the fuck is Jesús Garcia. I'm guessing not your everyday friendly cabby?"

Jesús laughed and clapped his hands together. Al standing behind him also smiled

"No, no I am not. I am in fact an official working on behalf of the government in conjunction with Al here who is a private operative working…"

"Jesus, and I mean the omnipresent being not you. Tell me exactly which part of the Feds or the CIA or NSA or whatever fucking acronym you work for and why the fuck you bastards are tailing me?"

The smiles dropped from his assailants faces, Jesús coughed and opened his hands, as if in appeasement.

"Alright, alright you deserve this. But it must remain within these four walls."

He nodded at the smartly dressed Latin American.

"Let's just say I'm the counter-intelligence man who makes sure the people in US government agencies behave themselves. We've been monitoring you since you landed in LA. We know you're here to do a hit on behalf of nefarious elements within our Federal Bureau of Investigation or the FBI. We know you're working with the private security firm Lodestar, out of London, as a mercenary for hire. We know you're ex-SAS, ex-Malay CID, and he have it on good authority that you're wanted for the murder of at least one police officer in northern Spain more than two decades ago. But what we don't know is who you are here to assassinate? Who?"

"I don't have to tell you anything."

"This we know. You can keep your mouth shut. I can speak to immigration, and we can have you deported before the close of play today. But my guess, and stop me if I'm going wrong here, is that you do not want this."

Jesús looked straight at him and then continued.

"The alternative is. You help us, you give us information we need to arrest these people, and we let you keep the money they've already paid you and maybe even your head."

He looked at the CIA man and thought intently. He'd worked in a similar role in the Far East and often agencies within the same government were fighting each other to get control of all the secrets. British MI6 were always trying to stick their noses into domestic affairs and influence counter insurgency in Malaya, even after independence. Having worked for the Empire and then the Malay police he'd seem corruption and power games really mess up the lives of a great deal of normal people on both the outside and inside. He now had to work out how to tell them just enough of what he knew without incriminating himself. OK they seem reasonable let's turn the tables on them, he thought, let's find out what they know. He reached into his pocket and pulled out a half-smoked panatela - a little bent but the wrapper was still sound. Al placed an ashtray on the table next to him - no doubt the coffee table he had gashed his mouth on. He nodded in thanks.

"Alright chaps. Why don't you tell me what you know, and I'll fill in the gaps."

Al looked skyward and swore and Jesús laughed and lit a cigarette.

"OK we'll do it your way. But believe me pal if I ain't getting the answers I want you'll be on the way home to a British jail in cuffs before your feet touch the ground. Comprende cabron?"

"Si gilipollas"

"And fuck you too Spaniard." Jesus took a drag from his cigarette and continued

"Here's what we know, you've been recruited by a rogue element within the FBI to take out a leading mob figure here in Los Angeles. Right so far?'

The Spaniard nodded and took a hit from his cigar.

"You've been recruited by an international security company in Britain. You're effectively a mercenary for hire?"

He waved his hand in a horizontal tilt from side to side as if to say, 'sort of'.

"You've been given a rifle, we're guessing ex-military issue, given a time and date of the hit and you've already been given a Presidential Pardon in writing should you get captured, which is probably not going to happen as the FBI are controlling the situation fully."

He noticed that they weren't aware of the Russians involvement in this, he'd keep quite on that one until he needed to do otherwise.

Al interrupted Jesús,

"He's right on almost everything apart from the fact that you ain't gonna be killing no mobster."

Jesús nodded and smiling said

"Unless you're intending to head down to Florida tomorrow your target will not be Paul Dragna."

The Spaniard looked at both men confused. Jesús continued

"The FBI have had a tail on Dragna for years. I've spoken to contacts who've told me he's been out of town for a month opening a bar on Miami Beach. He isn't due back for two weeks. So, who the fuck is your target?"

"Well gentlemen it's as much a mystery for me as it is to you. And Al what's your involvement with all this, are you playing both sides?"

"Don't change the subject. Al's been working for the Feds for years but what they don't know is that he also freelances for the bigger fish - namely us."

The room suddenly fell silent, there was a natural lull, the energy that had been expelled by all three men had gone - leaving an empty space. They all smoked or took a drink. The Spaniard stubbed out the last of his cigar; I better play this carefully he mused.

"OK yes, I admit I'm here to do a job. By the way it's my last one, a retirement piece so to speak. I know as much as you. I thought I was here to hit the Mob boss, do a good deed under the radar. Not strictly legal but not exactly the assassination of a President, is it? My main concern now is who the hell is trying to murder a girl I just met in Santa Monica?"

Both Americans stared at him, both failing to hide their confusion. Jesús spoke first.

"What are you talking about?"

"There's a dead girl in a Venice Beach bungalow. Luckily for my lady friend it's her roommate and not her. Not so lucky of course for the roommate."

Jesús looked at Al who shrugged. Al sparked up a cigarette. Exhaling as he spoke.

"Could it be a pissed off boyfriend? Maybe a rape or a burglary gone wrong?"

"No, it was a clean professional hit - an operation. They also think that they've been successful as the mark was a Latin woman and that's what they got. Just the wrong one."

He paused,

"And I'm fairly sure of one of the killers was that fat bastard in the army fatigues from the ghetto. The one we bought the rifle from."

Al stopped midway drinking a glass of whiskey. He put the tumbler down on the table, no coaster, in this immaculate place that meant he was rattled.

"Shit, that fucker's been supplying the Feds with unregistered guns for years."

"Unregistered?"

Jesús piped up

"Yes. No serial numbers, untraceable. Hey is your ladyfriend OK?"

"She's fine, thank you. She's hiding from everyone, including myself."

"Bueno, bueno."

The Spanish was starting to creep back into the CIA man's vocabulary, the stress was showing. He was trying to assess how much further to continue before he pulled called time on the whole operation.

"Alright listen up this is what we're going to do. I'd call LAPD and get that body recovered and the house closed as a crime scene. But I'm not going to release the identity of the gun dealer until this operation is over. We need to find out who the hell you're supposed to be taking out before the planned operation tomorrow."

Al stood up suddenly from one of the leather chairs and addressed the Spaniard.

"Wait, wait, amongst the papers and the Presidential Pardon I gave you in the diner yesterday wasn't there a photo of the target. I just assumed it was of Dragna but maybe, maybe it's the real target."

"And you're waiting until now to tell us? Where is it?" enquired Jesus

"Hey, I'm sorry, I only got a glance at the file after it was dropped off by that fat fuck Bradley. The folder is at the hotel."

"OK then, Al go with him back to the hotel in Santa Monica, get this photo and maybe we can work out who the fuck he's supposed to shoot."

After Jesus left. Both men stood outside Al's beautiful home in Torrance next to his beautiful Impala

"Hey Al, I'll follow you in that rust bucket down there."

He was pointing at the forlorn surfer's station wagon that he'd stolen from Venice.

"OK it's still rush hour, let's take the coast road north."

"And Al, I need to stop off on the way."

"Stop off where?"

"The ghetto, el barrio, I need to put a bad dog down."

"You gotta piece?"

"I got the rifle he sold me in the back of the car."

"Good let's get this shit done quick."

The Ghetto, South Central L.A.

They arrived just as the darkness had enveloped the sunset. This is what they needed anonymity, to see but not be seen. All was quiet on East 113th Street just off Wilmington Avenue in Watts. The residents were eating dinner, getting high or merely preparing for an evening of danger in the hood; whether they welcomed this as the perpetrators or feared it as the victims.

They'd parked the silver Impala along the side of a Baptist church, out of sight. The Nash Rambler they positioned right at the back of the parking lot, alongside a chain link fence and next to a dumpster. The surfer's passion wagon was in almost darkness, and it afforded a perfect view of the gun runner's dilapidated grey clapperboard house.

The Baptist Church looked similarly tired, and weather beaten. It was a faded dark red, with peeling paint flaking off to revealed bleached grey wood underneath. There was a large painted sign on the side of the building which read 'Jesus Saves Souls'. It looked like he was holiday in this neighbourhood, there was not a soul in sight. This being Monday they benefited from the fact it was the pastor's day off. The lot was vacant, and the lights out. The scene was perfectly set.

Al sat smoking in the front seat watching the house from the car's rear-view mirror. The Spaniard sat beside him, nursing the .32 Walther pistol he'd bought from the man they were waiting for. He spoke first,

"When you called him what did you say?"

"I said we got another job and need another weapon. He said he'd be back by dusk and so here we are."

Both men fell silent as they waited in the gloom for the gun runner to return to his home.

In the stillness of early evening; movement. A car trundled up the road and swung onto the driveway. Being a Spaniard who lived most of his life in Asia and London, he had no idea what make it was, it just looked old and battered with room in the rear for plenty of firearms (it was a rusty Studebaker Lark Wagon in 'Iridescent Copper Mist', now 'LA Smog Brown'). The large figure in the driver's seat suggested this was the man, the target. The car came to a halt and the engine juddered a little, as if trying to restart. Tappets need adjusting the Spaniard thought. Then the engine stuttered, like a death rattle, to a halt.

The driver opened the door and illuminated the inside of the cab. Large black man in green army fatigues. This was him. He got out of the car slamming the door shut and pausing to light a cigarette. He cupped it with his hands to light it. There was no reason why he should do this the air was still. Maybe he hailed from Chicago or the East Coast where the fierce winds caused smokers to shield their smokes. Not that either of the men in the aging Nash Rambler cared where this murderer hailed from.

The gun runner made his way inside the house and the two men exited the car. Glancing from side to side they crossed the road and rang a doorbell. A grumpy looking giant of a man answered. Al smiled,

"Hello Eddie"

The Spaniard with all his might hit the man smack in the mouth and like a prize fighter at the end of his career he was out for ten.

"Hey shithead wake up!"

The giant was strapped to a chair at the end of his basement shooting gallery. Al through a bucket of cold water in his face and he was shocked awake from his enforced slumber. His jaw was read from the Spaniards punch, and he had a cut on his forehead, likely from hitting the floor

"What the fuck."

He giant looked confused and glanced from side to side. Next to him stood Al, bucket in hand and at the far end of the basement was another man, the guy he'd sold the Remmington to and in his hands was, what looked like the same bolt action M40 rifle. Al bent down to the gun dealer's side and spoke slowly.

"Eddie, Eddie, Eddie. Looks like you got yourself into a slight situation here. Now we want to untie you, but we have a few questions first."

"Fuck You!"

The giant man in the green fatigues grunted before spitting onto the floor.

"If that's the way you want it."

Al walked away to one side and a shot ran out from the rifle just narrowly missing Eddie's enormous head and imbedding itself into the sandbags that were piled up against the wall behind him in his very own improvised shooting gallery.

"Jesus! What the hell!"

"Sorry Eddie but the man at the other end of that rifle doesn't like you, you tried to kill his girlfriend, and you murdered another woman instead."

"I don't know what you're…"

Al stepped back and another shot rang out, sending a plume of silica from the sandbags into the air.

"Shit OK, OK, look I was paid by that Jack Bradley motherfucker to kidnap a spic girl in Venice."

"And?"

Al stepped back to a position alongside Eddie. The man in the chair looked scared and was eyeballing both his interrogator and the shooter.

"And? Who's the target that Bradley wants to take out in LA? The reason you sold us that rifle."

"What? I don't know man. All I know is that I sold you the M40 and then Bradley hired me to get the girl. Honestly that's all I know."

"Another round for Eddie I think…"

"No stop, please don't!"

Al stepped back and the Spaniard pulled back the bolt on the rifle to cycle another cartridge. Eddie almost screamed!

"Wait, WAIT!"

"Let's see if he hits you this time Eddie."

The giant black man in fatigues screamed again.

"WAIT!"

The Spaniard at the other end of the gallery looked at Al who motioned for him to lower the rifle. Eddie exhaled deeply.

"Look he paid me a grand and hooked me up with this ex-marine called Harris. We were given an address and told to take the girl as some sort of insurance. But she wouldn't stop screaming and then Harris hit her to shut her up and then the gun went off. Look it was an accident; he shot her, and we got outta there quick. And that's it I don't know nothin' else."

He took a deep breath.

"The woman I didn't know but it was something to do with the son of a bitch who's firing that piece at me right now. Look man this ain't personal, it was just a job! I promise that's all I know. It was just a job."

Al tapped Eddie on the shoulder and placed an unlit cigarette into Eddie's mouth.

"Hey, Eddie that's alright, we're in the business, it's all just work."

Al helped him light the cigarette, despite him still being bound to the chair, and walked back towards The Spaniard. The large man inhaled and then exhaled deeply. The smoke drifted around the room mixing with the cordite from the rifle.

At the other end of the gallery the Spaniard was having a flashback to the jungles of Malaya twenty years before. He remembered taking out a CT who, decided to indulge in a cigarette. He'd waited for three days for this CT (Communist Terrorist) Colonel to make an appearance outside his jungle hideout. That'd been fun; lying in perfect stillness with your spotter on rough terrain, no cigarettes, only a little food and water, using amphetamines to stay awake, pissing into a rubber and shitting into paper bag that you'd take with you or bury. It was one of the most unglamorous roles in the army but was often hyped by civilians to be the most exciting. But whatever the process, what remained in your memory as the longest part of the operation was not the seventy-hour wait but the seven seconds of targeting and taking the shot. As if everything had slowed right down to make milliseconds feel like days.

After watching this Colonel, the in complete darkness of the jungle for a minute or two he could see the glowing end of the cigarette. As the cigarette end burned brighter, he knew the smoker was inhaling. If you followed that glow about three inches to the left or, as was in this case, the right you'd have the target's head, dead centre. Then it was merely a matter of taking aim, exhaling and then holding the breath and squeezing the trigger. The shot rang out, but he never saw the kill. What he did see was a shower of red sparks from the cigarette as it tumbled out of the mouth of the target. He still saw that shower of red-hot tobacco in his dreams. It was like a firework; a Catherine wheel spinning over and over. In his dreams he convinced himself he saw the destroyed face of the target, illuminated red by the dying embers of that cheap cigarette.

"So man, are you gonna untie me now?"

The Spaniard was suddenly jerked back to the present; a dank basement in South Central Los Angeles belonging to Eddie the gun runner. Al was leaning against the wall.

"Do you think we should untie him?"

BANG! The action on the rifle cycled, the dead cartridge was expelled and a new one loaded. BANG! Again, the rifle was cycled but there was no shot. It wasn't necessary. There were two bullet holes in the gun dealer - one to the head and one to the chest. His eyes were wide open and his mouth agape. As the Spaniard wiped down the desk he'd been leaning on and picked up all the empty shell casings he motioned towards Al.

"I guess that's all he had to tell us."

The Paris Blues nightclub - Inglewood -LA

The trumpet player was in full swing; jamming with apparent randomness but unbeknown to the audience he was pretty much following the musical score of a song written almost two decades before; albeit with his own unique interpretation. The saxophone break had finished, to rapturous and slightly drunken applause, the drummer had filled for a few bars and then it was the turn of the horn player. At the start of the solo, he lets out a few notes, as if in confusion, but it's all carefully planned. It is a harsh herald to the forthcoming solo which will take his audience on dizzying musical heights. Through the smoke, the lights and the electricity of the audience; the solo propels both the trumpet player and the crowd to new understandings of the word music. Well at least that's the theory.

They had secured a booth near the front door; the place was three-quarters full, not bad for a Monday night. After the shooting they'd sped out of the area and Al mentioned he needed a drink. Without asking where they would go the Spaniard nodded in silence. He hoped there would be people, noise, atmosphere. Anything to cleanse away what they and done. The smoke in the place did a lot to mask the smell of cordite and they both lit up cigar and cigarette respectively adding to the clubs already smoky fug.

The band played on through jazz standards such as Caravan, Ladybird, So What and Lady Be Good. The crowd lapped it up and the intensity of the music seemed to relax the men, that and the doubles of bourbon on the rocks. Although it was in Inglewood just off West Arbour Vitae Street, the crowd were a mixture of black, white and Hispanic, the jazz scene attracted an older audience; the haircuts were shorter than on Sunset. The sight of a Black and Latino man drinking whiskey in a booth and listening to jazz was not unusual. They blended in.

The waitress arrived with a third round and the music started to lull to a softer laid-back tune, Round Midnight. The Hispanic man raised a glass.

"You come here often after, as you Americans say, - *take out the trash*?"

The black man broke out laughing and they clinked glasses.

"Sorry, a little gallows humour I learnt in the British army."

Al smiled and laughed again.

"Yeah, I hear you there my man." Al lit another cigarette. "Fuck what a trip tonight was."

They both drank.

"But in answer to your question, yes, I come here often. Especially since my old lady moved on. I like the music, I like the booze, I like the women, and it beats lonely night back at my place in Torrance."

The act had changed, the new band were younger more Latino, as was the music. They were a quintet with sax, piano, guitar, drums and bass but there were no jazz standards here. They played Bossa Nova in a 4/4 beat; this was so much more the West Coast than the hard jazz of

NYC. Both men looked at each other and smiled, Al took a swig of his whiskey.

"This ain't my usual bag."

"Mine neither but then I grew up on the Duke and the Count."

"I hear you brother. Another?"

The Spaniard shook his head and took a hit from his cigar.

"I need a clear head for tomorrow. And let's not forget we need to get that photograph from my hotel room. We need to find out who the target is I'm supposed to take out before the actual event. Time is running out for both him but also us."

"Let's go."

The sax player started on another number but this time slower and with more feeling. The booth that the two men had sat in was now empty.

All that remained was a full ashtray, empty whisky glasses and a couple of dollars tip. The men had left to write history or to try and stop history being rewritten. It all depended on how you looked at it. They may be back but if they were they'd certainly be changed.

Hotel - Ocean Drive - Santa Monica

He wasn't surprised to see the room had been trashed. The door was ajar when they reached his floor and light spilled through the crack onto the wooden floor and the moth-eaten Turkish rug in the hall. The mattress had been upended, and the bedside light was still on but now sans shade on the floor. It resembled a drunken debutant who'd fallen over at the grand ball exposing her undergarments to all and sundry. That thought almost made him smirk as he began to pick up cushions, chairs, tables, the telephone and all sorts of hotel room constants that'd been strewn across the floor in the break-in. Al looked around, took off his small brown felt fedora and wiped his forehead.

"What a goddamn mess."

Together they went through the room putting things right and, more importantly, searching for what had been taken.

Al went downstairs to quiz the concierge, really just the night porter. The guy was probably way past retirement and looked like he spent most of his shifts asleep behind the front desk. Al had to rouse him from the arms of Morpheus, flashing his PI license. He rubbed his eyes and put on his glasses.

"Did you hear or see anything Sir?"

"Nah but my hearing ain't what it used to be son. Look people come and go at all sorts of hours here. It's that sort of hotel."

Al lit a cigarette offering the old man one.

"Thanks son. Hey, you need me to call the cops?"

"No. I doubt they could help me on this one."

"I used to be a cop you know."

The old man leaned back in his chair and blew blue smoke skywards.

"Really who with?"

"LAPD, West Bureau, Hollywood and Wiltshire back in the 30s and 40s. Boy was that a hoot."

"You fight in the war?"

"Nope I'd already fought with the Marines down in Nicaragua during prohibition."

Al reached across the front desk offering his hand.

"Well, Oorah Marine. I served too, 1st Division Korea. Staff Sergeant"

They shook hands. The old timer smiled, took another hit from the cigarette and put his reading glasses in his vest pocket. He had a mop of grey hair and a moustache, which looked like it'd been in and out of fashion a dozen times since he first grew it. He was short and wiry with a hint of a Californian tan, Al guessed he was in his mid-sixties.

"The name's Overton by the way. Look I'm just the part-time night porter; I cover when the other two fellas are away. I honestly didn't see a thing tonight, but I have been known to fall asleep on the job - not that it's exactly stimulating you understand."

Al smiled.

"Not the same as tracking down a suspect for murder."

"Yep, it certainly isn't."

The old man looked him up and down.

"The only thing I do remember about this evening was a foreign guy came in asking for the Limey upstairs. I told him he was out and the man took off."

"What did he look like?"

"Erm big, blonde and he talked like a Rusky."

"Russian?"

"Hey, I don't know Russian from shit but that's what he sounded like. And of course, there's that big fat midwestern fella in the blue suit that's visited but he ain't been here for a while."

Al knew he was talking about Bradley.

"Ok thanks Overton. Look if you remember anything else, here's my card."

"I'll certainly do that Sergeant."

Back upstairs Al found the room had been returned to almost normalcy.

"The old guy on the front desk told me they'll have a carpenter in tomorrow to fix the door. I'm guessing all the paperwork's gone."

"Most of it. The memo from the Feds, the photographs but hey they left my presidential pardon." He flashed the crumpled document at Al.

"Well, that ain't worth shit now. Look sit tight tonight and carry on as if everything is A-OK and I'll call tomorrow."

"Sure, thanks Al."

The Spaniard closed the door after the black detective left and lay on the bed. Al had mentioned a big blonde Slav been asking for him at the front desk. This had to be the Russians; this was getting far too messy and in less than twelve hours was about to get a whole lot messier!

Hotel, Ocean Drive, Santa Monica.

She came in the middle of the night like a dream. The hotel room was dark, and she gently knocked the door rousing him from his slumber.

"What are you doing here? You're supposed to be in hiding."

"I just needed to be with you tonight. I needed you tonight baby."

That word 'baby' was dragged out and long and slurred with her Nicaraguan accent, more like 'baybee'. She whispered sweet nothings in his ear as they edged over to the bed slowly entwining each other in caresses and kisses. The irony of being a Spanish man raised in Britain, first by a formal educational system and then by the British army was that he always felt a touch of ridiculousness when the passions of women, in particular Latin women, were raised. To him it seemed like a cliché, an archetype; that everyone born around the Mediterranean was hot headed, a passionate lover and incapable of holding together a stable government for more than a month or two. But just as he was thinking these thoughts his Latin temperament took over and he thought, aww fuck it.

Afterwards he dreamt of Malaya, he dreamt of his late wife. He was under white sheets looking into her honey-coloured eyes when a bright light started to obscure his vision. It was all encompassing; his eyes were blinded to it. The Californian sun was streaming into the hotel room through the blinds. He was alone and awake; the big day had arrived.

Hotel Room - American Empire - late 20th Century

The phone rang loudly causing him to swing his legs off the bed. That and the blinding Santa Monica sun, that was streaming through the window, caused him to feel a slight dislocation over his surroundings. He gripped the bedside table and took a drink from the glass on top - the water was tepid, not unlike his current state. He picked up the phone to end the incessant ring.

"Yes?"

"Hello Monsieur, my name is Mathieu Borel from Poncet & Cie. I understand you are expecting a transfer today?"

"I'm sorry it's early, you're who?"

He glanced at the clock it read 5.50am.

"Pardone Moi Monsieur. Sorry I forgot you're on the West Cost of America. It is just before three o'clock in the afternoon here"

He found an old cigar butt in the ashtray, lit it and exhaled blue smoke.

"That's alright. Sorry again please who are you?"

"Sir I am Mathieu Borel your private banker in Geneva Switzerland from Poncet Et Cie. I have to confirm a transfer of 50,000 US dollars into your account."

He smiled and took another hit of the cigar, the FBI, in their infinite wisdom, were transferring the remainder of the funds into his account before the hit had even taken place. He spoke again to the banker, wrapping himself in his bed sheet like a sarong, they went through security passwords and features again. He made sure he made changes to them and that no one, including the Swiss taxman, would be able to access his account.

"Monsieur I can assure you as a private bank in Switzerland your account is sacrosanct to us."

The banker said 'sa-cro-sanct' in three broken stages; worryingly as if the word was unfamiliar to his Swiss - French tongue - not dissimilar to the phrase *Jewish gold*. The banker continued,

"Sir a deposit of 50,000 US dollars has been placed into account number 35261889. Making your account a total of $100,000 US dollars. Now along with the other security features we need a new chosen word that you, and only you know, as to unlock the account in the future and release the funds for your usage and transfer funds and so on."

"A codeword?"

"Yes, Sir please"

"Erm, I don't know, hang on how about 'Misty'."

"And we're spelling that M - I - S - T - Y sir?"

"We are indeed."

"Well that all seems in order. It only remains for me to wish you a wonderful day Sir and I apologise once again for the very early timing of my call."

"Pas de problème Monsieur Borrel, pas de problème."

He placed the receiver back in its cradle. Misty, it had been the title of a song he'd heard the evening he first met his wife in Kula Lumpur's Police Club. Misty by Errol Garner.

He was musing this last thought when he saw a hand-written note lying right next to the phone. It read…

…*Thanks for last night. I'm heading back up to the hills this morning. Let me know what's going on when you can. Please stay safe - Love Maylin.*

He smiled, obviously that part of the night hadn't been a dream. There was a telephone number scrawled below the note. He dialled the number on the old Bakelite phone by the bed. It rang out for over a minute, and he gave up assuming she was probably on a cab on her way there now. He'd try later, after the business he needed to conduct had been concluded. That's if he was still around to.

Santa Monica - Come for the Beach & Stay for the Fun

There was no point in trying to go back to sleep there was too much on his mind. He had a big day ahead; try not to get killed by the Russians whilst working for some rogue FBI cell who're trying to kill a target who may, or may not, be a mafia boss and try to avoid ending up in a US army stockade for the next twenty years. Wow, yes, he really did have a rather hectic day ahead of him. He decided on a brisk walk along the California seafront and a good breakfast, or at least America's idea of one, then a shower a shave and off we trot to ice someone we've never met before for $100,000 dollars. Usual Monday then!

After taking a shower, very cool then very hot to wake him up, he left The Ocean Hotel. Overton the night porter was sound asleep on the front desk as befits a building painted the colour of spoiled seafood. He let the front door swing shut and made his way along the seafront paper coffee cup in hand. He was wearing the loose silk shirt that he'd bought to have dinner with Maylin. He'd paired this with a tight pair of slacks. His only exception to the laid-back fashionable nature of his attire was a pair of old tennis shoes; if he needed to run he wanted to be quick. The shoes had been bought by an ex-girlfriend who played tennis at The Hurlingham Club in London, right by the River Thames. She wanted him to enjoy a good game of tennis as much as she did, and they often played mixed doubles. To be honest he enjoyed her more than the tennis; still they were a good pair of shoes to be caught in when trying to stay alive

The wind blew across the sand and despite the blazing sun a weird fog started to drift inland from the sea. Everything went slightly hazy as he walked towards the Santa Monica pier; there was a strange silence in the air as if nature was expecting something to happen and just stopped all life for a particular moment. You could still hear the drone of traffic up on Ocean Drive but here the noise of seagulls, the waves crashing on the beach and even the people walking by seemed somehow muted. He sat down on a bench and took in the view of the dilapidated old pier. A once glorious structure jutting out into the Pacific saying to the world 'Fuck You! Look how frivolous we can be. We can construct a monument to pure pleasure, for pleasure's sake alone. God, we must be a nation to be feared'. It reminded him of the poem by Shelly 'Ozymandias' with America declaring itself to be 'King of Kings'.

Well, that was long ago and now things had definitely changed…

"Hello Spanish"

He swerved round and, as if from nowhere, sitting right next to him was Colonel Dimitry. He'd appeared out of the mist as if he was some sort of Soviet wizard, a magician straight out of the Kremlin's Magic Circle. He was resplendent in entirely inappropriate beachwear; a silver five-hundred-dollar suit for the beach with matching black Italian loafers. He didn't jump; he wasn't surprised.

"Colonel always a delight."

"Dimitry please."

"Colonel, how can I help you?"

"I see you're still here in Los Angeles."

"I just can't seem to tear myself away from the place. It's the people you know they're so, so friendly and open. It really is a whole different world from London and Europe."

"Yes, I like it here. Better than the Ukraine. People more pretty. Food and drink abundant. And as you can see tailors better than in Soviet Union." He pointed at his light grey suit with matching tie.

"Of course, very nice, perfect for the beach. It must have cost you a few roubles."

"I got lucky in Vegas last month. Suit is present from casino owners to me; courtesy of winnings."

The KGB man broke out laughing, genuinely laughing, probably at the absurdity of a devout communist winning big at blackjack on the Vegas strip. The Spaniard thought; we are all victims of circumstance, trapped in a place by good or bad luck or by the omnipresent will of a particular godhead - a Divine Architect.

The Colonel stopped laughing and coughed a few times, he then lit a cigarette. He exhaled smoke; much of which couldn't be seen as they were still surrounded by fog from the Pacific. The Colonel looked at him closely, as if sizing him up, he offered a cigarette, but it was refused.

"Sorry, I forgot you smoke only the cigar."

"Yes, Cuban if possible. Now there is a success story from the socialist world."

"We have many. First to put man in space, first to march into Berlin in 1945 and best caviar in the world."

"The later only available to the high echelons of the Party at home and the very rich here in the West."

"Yes, nothing is perfect, I am afraid."

There was a pause in the conversation only the sound of seagulls and the regular gentle rolling waves lapping the golden Californian sand. The Soviet lit another cigarette and turned to him.

"Spanish, we know why you are in Los Angeles. I beg you; you must not do this. You must leave California."

"Dmitry I'm sorry. It's too late I have a job to do. Unless you are planning to kill me now, I will complete this assignment."

"I thought you may say this. Then I have no choice but to tell you, you risk not only your life."

He looked at the aging Soviet warrior who was living the highlife in the dying rays of the Imperialist Western sun.

"What do you mean?"

"The girl Spanish, they have your girl."

Lake Cocibolca - Nicaragua - 1958

She was born into a privileged family just after the war. They'd only been wealthy for a generation and her father had been brought up poor; no shoes, dirt floors and leaving the school for the fields whilst still a child. He did though have a business brain and after a few years had his own fields, then farms then estates. He'd wisely invested in tobacco production and engineering (a chain of garages). Despite all of this he did not spoil his children, not Don Esteban. He them the experience of being a poorer Nicaraguan or Pinolero.

Her brothers had worked in the fields and then the garages. She herself had helped clean her father's office in the cigar factory in Granada. She'd also helped stack boxes and pack cigars, which she didn't like. The nails that sealed the cedar wood boxes had often caught on her fingers. What she did like to do was listen to the Lectores - the man or woman who read stories to the illiterate workers at the factory. They would broadcast the day's newspapers and sports results across the public address system or the latest blockbuster book to hit the Spanish speaking world. Often it was the classics, Shakespeare, Dickens and the ever-popular Cervantes novel Don Quixote.

For Maylin these wondrous stories had enthralled her. She'd been left with a love of literature, but also the newspapers; reporting on the turbulent nature of power in the country, an age of changing politics.

She'd started properly schooling at the age of twelve in the international school in Managua. Speaking American English in class and Spanish in the schoolyard. She dreamt of a life in politics, law, maybe even running her father's business. She was not going to be there merely for producing the prodigal grandchildren, the next generation in her father's empire.

The one thing that kept her lofty ambitions grounded was that every summer (the dry season) she spent with her grandfather. Whilst her rich friends whiled away December and January at their family beach houses, cruising through the Caribbean or exotic, holidays to Miami or Acapulco, she had a very healthy dose of reality.

Her grandfather lived on Ometepe, a volcanic island in the middle of Lake Nicaragua. Although years later would be a draw for tourists back then it was just a dirt-poor part of the countryside. Quiet with a few inhabitants farming tobacco, coffee and fishing. Along with her grandfather, this is what Maylin did during the dry season for almost ten years.

Her Abuelito or 'Abi' as she called him had grown up with almost nothing, a true son of the soil. Despite his son's huge success and business empire across the country the old man wasn't particularly interested. He was immensely proud of his family but for himself living in a mansion in the capital and driving a big American car didn't interest him that much. He often said

"There's only so many clothes you can wear and only so much food you can eat."

In early December a dilapidated diesel boat dropped the schoolgirl off at the island as her grandfather patiently waited for her by the dock. A small man - rich in Indian blood - with hands like shovels and a face weathered with the lines of almost seven decades working the land.

He lived in a small house surrounded by only a few acres set alongside the lake where he had easy access to the rich fishing grounds. He grew coffee and tobacco; some for sale at market and some for himself and this provided much more than he needed.

So here her education would begin. He taught her how work the fields, growing crops, feeding the livestock of chickens and pigs and most fun of all fishing the lake and hunting for shark. He taught her how to catch and gut all manner of livestock. She became adept at ending the life of an animal quickly and with mercy, she didn't shirk from gutting a dead pig, chicken or large fish. She found the process somewhat peaceful as if she needed to show reverence towards the dead animal that would be providing those still alive with sustenance.

The days started at dawn and finished at sunset with Saturday afternoon and Sunday's off. In their downtime they had climbed both volcanoes that dominated the island; Conception and Maderas. One was still active and the smaller, now extinct, was just a crater where a freshwater lake had formed. It was here at the later that they sometimes stripped off and swam in the serene warm water. She felt like she was swimming in the navel of the world. A surreal experience to be swimming in a lake inside a volcano on an island in a lake!

On other occasions her Abi had taken her to see the pre-Columbian statues that were littered across the island. Giant 10-foot carvings of lizards or birds or half-men and half-who-knows-what. She remembered one looked like a dragon sprouting up from the forest floor, covered in moss and lichen. Abi had lit a cigarette and patted the statue like a dog.

"I'm glad I'm here. It feels like I'm close to my ancestors, our ancestors."

She knew he was talking about his own mortality. Eventually becoming one of their number beneath the volcanic soil of the island; returning to the dust.

One day, Conception, the active volcano erupted and shook the small house. It was that memory of shaking that woke her up from her dream, as the car sped round a corner. It was pitch black and she was struggling against her bonds and trying not to panic. The last thing she remembered was leaving the hotel in Santa Monica. What she didn't know is that she was inside the trunk of a dark blue 1968 Ford Fairlane sedan as it sped up PCH.

The Burbs - Los Angeles - the big day

The safe house they'd chosen was almost equidistant from the target's location Downtown and the shooter's hotel in Santa Monica. Jack Bradley was given a choice of FBI owned buildings from which to plan the operation. He'd gone for the most discreet. It has a small two-bedroom single story set right on the edge of Carlson Park overlooking the old Ballona Creek. It was right at the dead end of the road; the slightly more run-down part of a very quiet neighbourhood; the one or two bars that were nearby shut before midnight. The property wasn't overlooked and there weren't many neighbours. It was close to the Inglewood Oil Field that put a lot of family's off settling too close for fear of explosions or pollution; not that you could escape the later in Los Angeles. Bradley was on the telephone in the kitchen.

"You got her right? Yeah? Good"

Bradley ran his hands through his hair as he listened to caller on the other end.

"OK yeah, she's in the trunk? Good. Right get back here now."

With that he slammed the telephone back into its cradle on the wall. It was one of those new designs with an extra-long coiled cable attaching the receiver to the body of the phone. So that housewives could chat with friends as they walked from the kitchen to the lounge popping diet pills and whiling away their lives. The kitchen itself indeed looked like it had been influenced by someone taking speed; bright yellow was the main motive with purple patterned tiles. Jack Bradley looked distinctly out of place as he smoked a Lucky Strike, looking dishevelled in a tan suit with a hideous orange tie. But he had a broad smile on his fat Germanic Mid-Western face. The telephone cord has wrapped its way around his feet, and he kicked it out of the way and went to the fridge grabbing a celebratory Coke from inside its vast white interior. He handed one to a scrawny looking man next to him.

"They got her and they're bringing her here. Make sure he knows we got her when you take the Spic to do the hit."

"Sure, sure. And after?"

"We'll dump her body in his car near the beach. Leave a gun with his prints on it. It'll look like a lover's spat gone wrong. That's not going to be a problem, is it?"

"Oh no that's the part of the job I like. I had lots of fun with her roommate down in Venice before I put a bullet in her head."

The wiry man smiled and took a pack of cigarettes out of his pocket, lighting a Kool's. Bradley grimaced and wafted away the smoke.

"How can you smoke that menthol shit Harris?"

"Three tours in 'Nam before I ended up instructing out of Pendleton Jack. That's hell of a lot of blacks I served with. You get a taste for their smokes."

Bradley smiled

"And their women?"

Harris smiled back

"Naw Jack, I was knee deep in *dep qua* boom boom girls, still am."

Harris had joined the Marines as a lifer in '58 and by '66 was a sergeant in-country. He'd served his three tours as both a spotter and a sniper. He'd been invalided out in '68 after his jeep hit a landmine and spent the next two-years working at Camp Pendleton as an instructor. On the side he had, secretly, begun working covert ops for the CIA, Feds and who ever would pay the most. Forays into SE Asia or Central America were fine by him; the pay far acceded that of the Corps and the perks were certainly better. Lots of local prostitutes, some good drugs and certainly no commanding officer giving you shit morning, noon and night.

He was a ragged man who looked ten years older than his thirty-four years. He had grown his hair since leaving the Marines and now also sported a dropping moustache. Coupled with yellowing teeth and bad skin this did not make for a pretty picture.

Bradley drained his Coke, crushing the can and hurling it into the trash.

"I'm gonna call the Spaniard and tell him you're on your way. Remind him that we got his girl, and he'll comply if he knows what's good for her, and him."

"Yes Sir. Glad to be back in the saddle sir. Nothing like doing your job on home soil."

Bradley's mouth formed a thin smile, whilst his eyes said distain.

"Just make sure you do your job Harris, and that Spanish Limey fuck does his."

"Harris smiled back with small snake eyes and exhaled blue menthol smoke and quietly spoke."

'Oorah boss, Oorah.'

OCEAN HOTEL - SANTA MONICA

He was smoking a large cigar he'd purchased the day before in the bay window of his hotel room looking out across the sunlit bay of Santa Monica. It wasn't' quite nine-thirty; far too early for this quality of smoke but it was a big day. The label on the cigar said Cuesta Ray and there was a picture of a pretty Spanish girl; painted from the side like a Victorian cameo. It was a truly great cigar; a pyramid about seven inches long and tapered to a point which he'd cut off with his Taramundi knife. It was a thick gauge of almost ¾ of an inch and the smoke was beautifully light and tasted of sweet coffee and vanilla. Plumes of smoke swirled around his head and towards the ceiling gently twisting out through the open top window.

He'd run out of Cubans and decided to purchase this yesterday. It was a small store round the corner and the shopkeeper behind the counter told him this was the best you could buy outside of Cuba. It was Florida rolled with Cuban grown seed from the Dominican Republic. He had purchased a variety of different sizes from the large humidor to the side of the counter. The small man smiled as the Spaniard smoked a small cigarillo,

"This is good." He exhaled smoke "Very good."

"I'm glad you like it." He replied, "Those communists in Cuba don't know all the tricks about making great cigars."

As he stood there in the hotel room, dressed in a two-piece suit in dark sunglasses, sneakers for ease of exit from the crime scene, he pondered the forthcoming events and tried to find a quiet space in his mind to capture thoughts about the events that were to unfold. The nicotine coursing through his veins helped him do that. He took another draw on the cigar, letting the smoke curl inside his mouth before blowing it towards the bright blue pacific.

This moment of peace had been inspired by the knowledge of who was holding Maylin. She may not be safe, but she was at least alive. That corpulent ass Bradley had called him telling him they had the girl and hoping it would encourage him to finish the job properly and not skip off with the government's hard-earned cash. If he tried to exit the country; she'd be dead, and he probably wouldn't make it past the check-in-desk at LAX.

Although he'd only known Maylin for a few days, less than a week, he'd found her to be a truly unique individual. She ignited something within him that'd been dormant for years since the murder of his wife. This wasn't infatuation and it was far too early to be love but there was a connection, which for him was a rare find. The thought of her not being with him, let alone killed, chilled him to the core.

"Just do the job OK Limey?"

"I promise you if there's a hair on that girls head that's out of place Bradley…"

"Alright, alright. Shut up and listen I'm sending over the spotter. He's gonna drive and you're gonna focus and get the job done."

"Is it that black private eye?"

"Nah I don't think I can trust that fucking ex-cop nigger again. This is a white guy called Harris, a former US Marine. He'll be there by ten, be ready OK."

The phone went dead.

Now as he smoked and looked out of the window, he readied himself for what had to be done. Done to this poor target; of which he had no knowledge and done to people like Jack Bradley. Oh, he knew what he had to do. He took another draw on the cigar and waited for the phone call from the front desk. Blue smoke wafted out across the bay.

Lodestar Operations, Whitehall, London

Four days earlier Thomas Fraser was doing the very same thing: staring out of a window and blowing blue smoke, this time cigarette, up towards the ceiling. Although it didn't funnel out of an open window across a beautiful Pacific Bay, this was London after all, wet and cold in February not sunny California. Instead, it rose upwards pooling and disappearing into the rapidly yellowing Georgian ceiling of the Palladian building.

The view he gazed upon was also slightly more monochrome than that of West Coast California. His office looked out across Whitehall, the real home of the British establishment. Here the civil service had run the Empire for almost two hundred years despite what governments came and went.

Fraser's view from the single glazed window, muddied by rain driving, was of another Georgian building which housed his gentlemen's club; of which his family had been members for generations. The Whitehall Club was not as old or regal as some, but it was a mark that one had arrived in the upper echelons of British society. He loved the fact he was a member; he loved the fact that it was almost impossible for just anyone to join (usually through family or the old boy network). But most of all he found it propped up his own lack of self-confidence.

He'd been a poor student at boarding school he'd failed to secure a place at university and just scrapped through officer training at Sandhurst. The only reason he hadn't been drummed out of his regiment was thanks to the cache of his father's name. The elder Fraser was the military tactician's tactician.

Despite his all his shortcomings what Fraser was very good at was winning friends, influencing people and glad handing those in the know. In fact, if they were handing out medals for brown nosing or kissing ass, he'd he a four-star-general by now.

He inhaled deeply from the Dunhill cigarette in his hand and thought about the lunchtime menu at his club. God, he hoped they didn't have Brown Windsor soup as a starter again. This was about as appetising as it sounded, a meat soup of origin unknown. Some mused that it's sourced from the sewage outlet at Windsor Castle - the Queen's regal weekend retreat.

The intercom on his desk buzzed loudly and his receptionist's voice broke the quiet stillness.

"Mr Collins for you Major Fraser."

He's kept the title of Major, despite not being in service anymore, again it bolstered his somewhat shrivelled ego. He groaned and walked over to the intercom.

"Thank you, Caroline, please send him in."

Fraser taped the ash into an enormous cut glass crystal ashtray. He turned towards the door as it opened and there stood a stony-faced man who looked like he'd faced a thousand foes, which probably wasn't far from the truth. He was of medium height but built like the proverbial brick shithouse. His light grey suit couldn't disguise his forty-six-inch chest, seventeen-inch biceps and thick neck. Despite this he didn't look like he carried an ounce of fat. There were scars on his hands and a nasty one down his neck. His hair was short (ideal for hand-to-hand combat) and set deep into his skull were his eyes, a cold grey blue. There was some white and grey to the sides of his hair but the top remained jet black. He was in his mid-forties and looked like he would win any bar fight he was challenged to; being an ex-military policeman, a retired regimental sergeant major, a veteran of WW2, the Korean war and Malaya Emergency this wasn't a man to be messed with. He looked exactly what he was, a professional soldier for hire a Merc. Fraser stepped forward hand extended.

"Collins, good to see you."

"Sir."

A monotone reply, not questioning just accepting.

"Yes, well, can I get you a drink?"

"No Sir, thank you."

Fraser laughed awkwardly and rubbed his hands together.

"Well, I'm sure you don't mind if I do?"

Fraser poured himself a large Scotch and water

"No Sir please, after all it's your office ain't it Sir."

"Yes quite."

Collins had a Thames estuary accent, he'd been born right by the river in London near Rotherhithe Docks, but he'd not lived there since he went into the army as a teenager. Despite this the South London Bermondsey tone had never left his voice, he liked it, as many found it somewhat threatening. Collins purposely emphasised his accent with upper class idiots like Fraser. On one hand it gave them a sense of superiority over him, which was what he wanted them to think; *oh dear he's just poor working class cannon fodder*. But on the other it also made them much more afraid of him and more malleable when it came time to negotiate his fee. The room fell silent, Collins continued to stare at Fraser without saying a word. Fraser pipped up.

"I understand you've been out in Oman, fighting for the Sultan?"

"Yes Sir, he's been having a little trouble with the Commies Sir. They've got no respect for the Profit you know."

"The Profit?"

"Yes, the Profit Sir, may peace be upon him, they show him no respect."

Collins inwardly smiled, he knew this upper-class twat had no idea he was talking about Islam and the rise of communism in the Middle East. He spent the last eighteen months protecting an aging Monarch, then his son, the prince, following a coup.

"Mind you they pay handsomely the Arabs do Sir."

"Yes, yes quite. Which brings me to our meeting today. As you are at somewhat of a loose end I wondered if you'd mind tying up a few loose ends for the company?"

"Well Sir I'd be happy to."

Collins pulled out a silver packet of American cigarettes and began to tap the box filter side down into the palm of his hand.

"For the right price Sir, obviously"

"Of course, of course you'll be well compensated for your time. It's an in and out job stateside. You'll be there no more than forty-eight hours. You see I've got a joint American operation in the works and I'm not sure I can guarantee that the Yanks will uphold their part of the deal. I need a man who can get things done, look after the interests of Lodestar, I'm sure you understand."

Collins continued to tap the packet of cigarettes.

"Well now Sir, you've piqued my interest, please tell me more."

Both men laughed and Fraser offered him a Dunhill, but Collins shook his head. He took out one of his own cigarettes and let Fraser light it with his gold Dupont. Collins exhaled skyward; the cigarette looked like a tiny lollypop stick in his gigantic hands.

LOS ANGELES - SANTA MONICA FREEWAY

The car made its way towards Downtown without either speed or haste. The hit was scheduled for one o'clock and it was a little after ten, the sun had just started to warm up the concrete. The air outside the car was still cool in the early morning and a breeze fluttered into the car as they motored along. They were riding in the same dark blue 1968 Ford Fairlane that had played host, or more correctly prisoner, to Maylin some three hours previously. Her location was known only to the man driving the car and not his passenger. Taking her place, in the trunk of the car, was a long canvas tool bag and inside wrapped in an old bedsheet was the M40 Remington sniper rifle and a box of 7.62 NATO cartridges.

Harris had the wheel of the car, and he drove just below the speed limit. They were in no rush, and he had no wish to attract attention. He was laid back in his seat and his free hand cradled a bottle of Coke as the car wafted down the highway. His eyes were hidden by a pair of yellow tinted Aviator sunglasses. This plus his awful baggy brown suit and Mexican Zapata moustache made him look like a plain clothes Vice cop who's seen far too much action. He smiled at the Spaniard; knowing that they had his girl and were prepared to do anything to ensure the job was done. He regarded him like a cat regards a half dead mouse trapped underneath his paw. The mouse stared straight ahead, showing no emotion. The Spaniard would reveal his cards when he was good and ready and when he knew nothing going to happen to Maylin.

They named it the I-10 back in the 1950s and stretched from California all along the bottom of the country through Arizona, New Mexico, Texas, Louisiana, Mississippi, Alabama and finally Florida. The grand plan was to link ocean to ocean, the Pacific here in the West through to the Atlantic in the East. Well, that was the plan, this section of the road was a huge smooth concrete path that snaked from the beach right up into the centre of LA. He glanced in the nearside wing mirror and saw a silver shark of a car tailing them; he prayed it was Al in the driving seat.

Before Harris had picked him up he'd tried, in vain, to get hold of either Al or Jesus. Both their numbers had rung out; he'd tried the CIA city office, but a very nice lady just told him.

"He's out all day today won't be back until tomorrow, Sir. Can I take a message?"

He gave her his name and the address of the hit and hoped that Al or Jesus would get the message. He prayed that the 'out all day' meant that these two, plus hopefully a battalion of Marines (Royal or US he wasn't fussed) would be waiting for them downtown outside this restaurant La Romana. Harris had told him it was on Seventh, just after Main, and he remembered it all. It was his military training, it never left you. Like his ability to sleep. Most old soldiers were trained to fall asleep at the drop of a hat. Literally ask them to close their eyes and get some rest and they were gone. After many years out on patrol one never knew when you were likely to get your next chance to close your eyes without having your head blown off. Today though, he wasn't in the mood to sleep.

The car drove through Mar Vista, Culver City, Jefferson, University Park; all of these looked the same to him a wide highway, lots of concrete buildings and sunshine everywhere - sunshine and smog. The traffic was light, pick-up trucks, a few buses, commuters in a myriad of vehicles from the 1940s up to the present day. It would never cease to amaze him how many people in this country drove cars, they were everywhere and in such large sizes. In Britain he'd only ever owned a couple of cars, most of them small rusty and unloved.

The car suddenly sped off the freeway and sharply took an exit it looked like it had pretty well overshot. The Shooter inhaled sharply then swore, the driver laughed. The silver shark that was following them drove past the exit. Harris leaned ion toward him.

"Just making sure we ain't being tailed."

The car had merged onto the 110 and then sharply turned off the freeway and onto a side road, turning right then right again and driving under the freeway itself and heading Downtown. They passed the homeless bums, who lived under the bridge, sheltering from the sun and the cruel hand life had dealt them. Men with long beards who'd served in numerous wars around the globe vacantly starred at the car, from under faded and ripped velvet fedoras or wrapped in blankets Indian style.

After a few minutes the car began to slow down and turned off into a side alley and then behind a large brown 1920s building. It was high for British standards, but this was the land of the skyscraper so eleven stories, not so much. He could see the ground floor was given over to mostly retail outlets, there was a travel agent

'Come Visit the Islands' the poster with a beach and blue ocean said. It didn't say which islands, just 'the islands' was enough to entice fat tourists to part with their hard-earned dollar to taste something tropical and complain about how it wasn't quite as nice as home in Poughkeepsie. There was a restaurant and what looked like some kind of bank or loan company on the far corner - that could be an issue with security guards and guns he thought. They were in the parking lot to the rear, obscured from public view. The car came to a halt and the driver engaged the parking brake. He turned towards his passenger.

"OK we're here. You know what you gotta do. I'm gonna point him out to ya'll to make sure you get the right guy then once it's over we get the fuck outta there like a scald cat."

Harris' accent revealed his dirt-poor Appalachian roots in the Blue Mountains of North Carolina. The stress of the job at hand caused him to drop into that familiar mother tongue. Not that the shooter noticed, they all sounded American to him, rich poor Southern or Northern, it was his first time stateside and the old adage about two countries separated by a common language was never truer.

"You got that? Comprende Amigo?"

Remember keep calm, don't bite, you have Maylin's safety to think about. The Spaniard kept reminding himself to push away thoughts of anger against this man and the situation he was being forced into. As his old commander in the Far East would remind him *'Keep your powder dry old boy, keep it dry until you're ready for action'* - using an old military adage.

Effectively, know when to strike and when you do strike hard. He looked through Harris.

"Yes of course, I'm ready."

Harris looked back at his shooter, he knew a thousand-yard-stare when he saw one. You don't spend years in the jungle and not know when a man is beyond the realm of fear and worry or at least has spent too much time fighting to fear or worry about anything - except the job at hand. He'd have to keep an eye on this one; this British Spanish, whatever the fuck he was, sniper was not a man to be messed with. Better put a bullet in his head as soon as the target's been shot, he thought. He smiled at the Spaniard with yellow and broken crocodile teeth.

"You better be ready Amigo."

They both got out of the car and headed towards the trunk for the equipment.

The Garment District - Los Angeles

Meanwhile an almost mint, galactic silver 1966 two-door Chevy Impala was racing up and down the side roads of Downtown trying to find a dark blue 1968 Ford Fairlane he'd been tailing since Santa Monica. Al was convinced that neither of them had seen him. He'd picked up the car a few streets down from the hotel and had stayed a few vehicles behind. He was certain they didn't know they were being tailed. He did this shit for a living, and he was pissed that he'd been made. It was either that or this greasy looking mother fucker who was driving the car in front was just making sure he wasn't followed. Well, it worked, and Al missed the exit.

He knew they were headed Downtown but he didn't know specifics. After the apartment had been turned over someone had made off with all the files. He figured it'd be best just to tail the Spaniard until they hit the target. He pulled over to the sidewalk and jumped out of the car. He fished around in his pockets pulling out loose change and fed it into a payphone that stank of cheap beer and a week's worth of piss in similar volume. Not that he noticed, it was almost twelve and the assassination was due to take place at one. Coins spilled on to the floor in his haste. He hurriedly fed the slot and dialled the number firstly to the local CIA office and then when he had no luck there to Jesus' home number in Santa Barbara. Five rings then an answer,

"Hello."

"Hi it's Al."

"Al? I'm sorry who?"

"Al, come on man, from…"

He suddenly twigged this wasn't Jesus but maybe another CIA man or a FED or another agency that had a three-letter acronym.

Al coughed and changed his tone.

"I'm sorry I think I may have the wrong number. I'm looking for my friend, he drives for Walnut Cabs."

"What did you say your name was sir?"

With that Al slammed the phone back into its cradle. He realised that the voice on the other end was a government one. Jesus was being either detained or monitored by the Feds or both. Fuck, he had to find out where the hell the Spaniard was before things got hot and people got shot.

The Apartment - Downtown

The men climbed the stairs from the rear of the building. There was an entrance at the front but as the old saying goes *discretion is the better part of valour*, or more rightly keeping yourself hidden from the nosey old bitch on the second floor made for an easier operation. Harris took the lead whilst the Shooter followed behind carrying the rifle and bullets inside what looked like a dark grey plumber's bag. The bag didn't look heavy, and he barely felt the weight of the M40, its tripod and ammunition. He was high on adrenalin and cortisol; the usual fuel that kept soldiers going up and over the top of the trench. It also helped when you got shot, numbed the pain and helped you fight back. Not that he was planning to get shot. He looked at the space between Harris's shoulders as they climbed the stairs and thought he'd be happy to put a bullet into this odious little man. His stomach was tight as drum, and he was beginning to sweat.

What his actions would be when push came to shove, and he had to wield the rifle and take the shot, he didn't know. He didn't want to shoot someone he didn't know, for a reason he wasn't privy too and for a cause that he certainly had no vested interest in. Sure, when he was told it was strictly a military government job, and he was going to get paid handsomely to take out a mobster; that seemed pretty good. He'd pay off the mortgage on the London house and maybe get some sort of normal job to supplement his meagre army pension. Whatever normal was.

Apartment seven, third floor was set in an unremarkable space. The hallway outside was tired and old with scuffed floors, walls painted in a hue of despair brown. It looked like it hadn't been decorated since the 1930s. Things didn't get rosier on the inside. There was no furniture, bare wooden floors and bits of old newspapers scattered around, he guessed this had been used as underlay for a carpet that was now long gone. He looked at Harris who was busy closing the front door.

"How did you manage to get the apartment?"

"We had three to choose from. The building's old and the owner doesn't want to decorate. They're throwing up new houses in the suburbs and nobody wants an apartment in Downtown LA. So, we had our pick and the one we got gives you a perfect view of the restaurant and the target. Take a look."

Harris pointed towards the window and motioned for him to come over. It was open but the blinds were angled as to make them invisible to the streets below. He could see the red and black of a long awning outside with tables and chairs beneath so the customers could imagine that they were in some piazza in Milan and not the hot dry pavement on the West Coast. It was starting to get busy, and people were taking up seats outside. A woman in large sunglasses and a broad black sunhat was drinking water from a wine glass. He couldn't really see but knew that there would be moister forming on the outside of that glass in the LA heat, causing water to drip on to the table, maybe even her lunch. She was very pretty with dark hair, maybe Latina, maybe Italian. He hoped she finished eating before he began his work.

Above the entrance to the restaurant was a gleaming red plastic awning with the name La Romana emblazoned across it in black. The message could not have been clearer - make no mistake this is an Italian restaurant! Beneath this awing would be the ideal location to take the shot on the intended target. The sun was high in the sky and at its current angle those beneath the canopy would be lit up like rabbits in the headlights. A more perfect set up for assassination one couldn't ask for. He glanced at his watch and then at the old brown clock on the wall. Both read around 12.25pm, about half an hour until go time. He needed to set up his kit, he needed to calm himself and he needed to get ready for the job at hand.

Garment District Downtown Los Angeles

The sun was at its zenith and the smog was starting to build up as was the norm in LA. Al was stood near the telephone booth smoking cigarette after cigarette, pacing up and down and trying to work out where the shooting was going to be and who the target was. He had just over half-an-hour to get there but he had no idea where there was. He walked back up to the booth pulled out his black cop's notebook and pumped change into the slots. He punched an LA number and waited, the phone rang once, twice, three times, four, he went to put down the receiver when the ringing finally stopped. and a deep voice spoke.

"Yeah what?"

"Hey, hey is that, Jack? Look it's Al here…"

"Where the fuck have you been shit heel?" He interrupted.

"Calm down man I'm trying to help you here."

"Calm down, calm down? It's the big event jack-off and I have seen neither hide nor hair of you for two days. Where've you been Al? I've been leaving messages for you Al. Why the fuck didn't you get back to me Al?"

Al loosened his tie some more, at this rate it'd be dragging on the ground, and took a hit off his half-smoked cigarette. He was hot and tired, sweat patches had formed around his shirt armpits and he mopped his forehead.

"Look I've been busy with another client but I'm all on board now Jack, I'm here right now. How can I help, tell me where the action's taking place?"

Al heard laughing down the line, as if the receiver was taken away from the voice on the other end. The laughing stopped suddenly Jack came right back on the receiver.

"I don't know who you are, I don't know who you're working for but lose this fucking number moon cricket."

With that the line went dead. Al cursed swore and smashed the receiver back into its cradle again and again. A bum walked past with a huge bushy grey beard beneath an old straw hat. He quickly crossed the road with his shopping cart full of trash. His wide bloodshot eyes growing more alarmed at the angry black detective. Al cursed again and rested his head against the pay phone. He knew he'd fucked up; he knew that Bradley and his rogue FBI unit wouldn't have trusted this ex-cop turned PI as far as they could've thrown him but their suspicions must have been further raised when he disappeared from their radar two days ago. He thought he never needed to contact them again. In this he was wrong and how wrong was obvious.

Al leaned against the payphone and checked his watch 12.36pm - he had less than thirty minutes to find the location of the shooter. Think, think he told himself. A group of women exited a large warehouse building opposite and all began to light up cigarettes and chat. Some were wearing house coats and others a tabard or bib all in a powder blue. He randomly thought the shift must be changing, they're sewing machinists. The new shift started to arrive, and they were beginning to put their hair up and pull out on their uniforms. It was a perfect moment of community for these women to chat and gossip at the end of a shift or before had begun. Some of them were Latina, some poor white others black or who knows. A police car drove past slowing down to wave at the women. Obviously, a regular patrol in the neighbourhood and the women all waved at the car smiling. They knew the driver; he was an older cop with slate grey hair and a moustache. Al thought he even looked too old to be on the force and that's when a thought hit him like a bolt from the blue; *fuck I know where the hit's gonna happen or at least I know someone who knows.*

OCEAN HOTEL - SANTA MONICA

The bald man who was the day clerk at the hotel had just made a batch of fresh coffee for customers in the machine and was sitting down to enjoy a cup himself when the phone rang. He picked up the black receiver.

"Ocean Hotel, Roy speaking. Yes, yes alright sir. Now just let me take a look."

The man put done the telephone and made his way over to the bank of numbered cubby holes behind the front desk. They contained the spare keys for each room and was the location staff placed letters and mail for longer term residents. He returned with a piece of paper.

"Yes, I can see my colleague left a note right here for yourself sir. Would you like me to read the address for you? Well yes, I certainly can."

After reading the address out loud he took a sip of coffee.

"Will there by anything else sir, hello sir hello?

But the line was dead.

The Apartment - Downtown

When he was a young man the cortisone and adrenalin coursing through his body would have had time zipping past like a train in the night. Things had changed in the twenty-five-years since he'd killed for the first time; the Spanish police, those *cerdos* who'd murdered his family. On the streets of Madrid and in the jungles of SE Asia his heart would be beating and his attention acutely focused when he was entering dangerous situations. But the years of experience, as a soldier, then a cop and now a mercenary had hardened him. He had positioned his mind into an assassination or sniper mode. He'd begun to slow down everything he did, everything he experienced and his reactions to both. He would be as calm as the Dalai Lama when he came to take that shot; ensuring he hit what he was aiming, for and the target stayed down. Every fibre of his being would be focused on the job at hand. He would become the Zen marksman, the deliverer of death from a place of calm, hence the phrase 'a stone-cold killer'.

He'd taken off his jacket and rolled up both sleeves. His rifle was now out of its bag and set up on a small low table that had been pressed up close against the window. It was mounted on a bipod and fitted with the scope. He would have liked more time to prepare for the hit, but he'd already had more time than in the field of battle. He'd zeroed in the gun when he was at the mocked-up shooting gallery back at the arms dealers' house in East LA. He'd taken a shot into a target then adjusted the telescopic sight to where that bullet had hit. It was crude but very effective. In the last few minutes he'd checked for wind, there was none, the sun was out and it was getting hot. He'd checked the sight looking right into the doorway of the Italian restaurant and he watched customers coming in and out; mentally preparing himself to take the target down with a headshot. This US army issue M40 was similar to a weapon he'd used before in the Middle East. It was going to be vastly overkill; the rifle was good for more than a thousand yards and maybe there were just over a hundred between his window and the restaurant entrance opposite.

He leaned back into his chair and took stock of the situation. He really didn't want to kill this target; he had no idea who the middle-aged man was, even if he still had the photograph the FEDs game him, he'd be none the wiser. He strongly objected to being forced in this role, but he was left with little choice they had Maylin, and he needed to ensure her safety. Despite this he promised himself that when he saw an opportunity to right this situation, he was going to take it.

"Getting yer-self ready to take the shot? You gonna need a spotter boy or will you be good from here? I mean you're practically next to the target."

Behind him leaning his chair against the wall and smoking a cigarette was Harris. He smiled and began to laugh.

"You sure you can hear me, Pancho? Are you gonna need some help?"

He rested the rifle and turned to the scruffy ex-soldier behind him.

"No, no I'll be fine, I've been doing this for a couple of decades."

Harris had another bottle of Coke and took a swig.

"You better be if you want to see that fine Mexicana lady of yours."

Harris smiled and raised his eyebrows. He'd managed to get cigarette ash down his awful brown suit and even with this level of bating he came across as somewhat pathetic. The Spaniard smiled inwardly refusing to rise to the taunts and returned to his Zen like state. He took another look through the scope, one eye closed, the target was illuminated brilliantly in the midday sun. The clock on the wall read 12.46pm

Garment District Downtown Los Angeles - 12.51pm

The silver Chevy screeched around the corner cutting the cub and narrowly missing a fire hydrant. Its long silver nose bounced up and down as Al tried to wrestle the steering wheel straight. He was following the route of Highway 10 but had to try and get back over to 7th, which was a good twelve blocks over. Shit, a dead end, he swung the wheel again and turned right then left to get back on track. A pretty, silver hub cap pinged off the front wheel and went spinning down the road hitting the sidewalk and coming to rest against the side of a Mexican restaurant; not that LA noticed.

Now he had the address he had less than ten minutes to get over there before the assassination took place and he was dammed sure he wasn't going to miss it. He owed that to his boss, Jesus, the Spaniard and himself. Al was a guy that got the job done, he kept repeating himself as the car swung around another corner. He narrowly missed a group of men who were emerging from a bar and spilling out onto the sidewalk and road - probably shift workers from one of the nearby warehouses a few beers after clocking off or clocking on. They swore *Maricon* and 'yer fuckin' bum' at him and threw their cigarettes in his general direction. He didn't register this at all he was focused purely on his goal to stop that assassination and his destination, La Romana Restaurant, 1pm, Tuesday 9th February, Apartment 7, Third Floor, 111 7th Street Downtown just after Main. He glanced at the address in his hand, then at his watch, six minutes to go. He could make it, he would make it, he hoped.

La Romana, 7th Street Los Angeles - Lunchtime.

A large black sedan pulled outside the restaurant, it wasn't a great location wedged in between the Fashion District and Skid Row but people came from all over the city to try the pasta. There was something special about the fare on sale at this establishment, after all hadn't it been here for thirty years. The owner Salvatore 'Sal' Viotto had come out to LA with his wife back in '41. He'd been scared that after the US joined the war that the Nazis would try and bomb New York. He gave up the lease on his café in Little Italy and headed west. Back then he'd been amazed at what he could rent right in the centre of LA, and for so little. They settled in the heart of Downtown and become rightly famous for their marinara sauce and the pasta: all made by hand in their own kitchen. All the Jews and Italians who'd headed out to LA from the East Coast were dying for some of that authentic Italian cooked food that was so hard to find in the City of Light. But what Salvatore and his wife Maria knew that the competition didn't; always make pasta dough with ice cold water; like back in the old country and use the freshest ingredients. So, their success story was born and named La Romana after his father's birthplace in the Italian capital. All sorts had come to taste this perfect piece of Italian NYC in the heart of downtown LA: movie actors, directors, musicians, politicians. Only a week ago the state governor Ronald Reagan came for dinner with his wife Nancy; both of whom Sal remembered used to be stars of the silver screen. These days Sal took a backseat to the operation with sons, daughters, and in-laws of all kinds helping out. But the restaurant was still always full at lunch and dinner six days a week.

All four doors on the black sedan opened almost simultaneously and six men stepped out; it was a large American saloon, about four years old, and was built like a battleship. Of the group four men were older aged between around forty and sixty and dressed smart casually with jackets and trousers and one smaller man with a black fedora. The other two men were in their thirties: much bigger built like the proverbial brick shit houses. These were the bodyguards. All six were of dark Latin complexions and looked like they were here on business rather than pleasure.

The group were met by a young dark-haired man, in a clean white shirt and black tie, by the entrance to La Romana. He began to usher them into the restaurant underneath the red plastic awning, he was obviously the maître d'. The two young and bulkier men, were looking around and encouraging them to go inside but the small man in the fedora motioned towards a table outside, set back from the road underneath a red and black umbrella. They at first started to object but relented as he shook his head and pointed at the table. This was obviously the leader of the group.

They all sat down, and the small older man removed his black hat, smoothing down his sparse hairline. He was very small and very brown, looking like he lived in the sun or had at least done in the past. He kept on his dark sunglasses, despite being in the shade but took out a packet of cigarettes, one of the bodyguards pulled out a silver lighter, helping him light it. He was soon puffing away and perusing the menu in a cloud of smoke. He glanced up briefly as the midday sun glanced off the windows of the building opposite. He was laughing at something one of his companions had said.

Then suddenly a gunshot, then two more, there was panic. The tables and cutlery went crashing to the floor as the two bodyguards dived onto the small man, pulling out pistols, they were trying to protect him. Then there was silence, utter silence in the middle of Los Angeles, that was a strange thing for the City of Lights. It was strange and unnatural for a burgeoning mega city. There were no blaring horns, no people shouting, the droning traffic seemed to quiet down to nothing. As if the gunshots had cleared the air for some tumultuous event yet unknown. It was strange and unnatural.

The Apartment - Downtown

Al's car screeched to a halt in the backlot behind the building, the force of his car kicking up rubbish and old newspapers. He jumped out not bothering to close his driver's door and took the steep steps, two at a time, bursting through the backdoor and hit the stairs running. He had just made the first landing and swerved round to take the next set of stairs he had made it to the second floor, one more floor to go. Again, taking the stairs two at a time, he almost tripped over the top stair but recovered, checking his watch. Fuck he hoped it was slow; it read three minutes after one. He pulled his gun and ran down the corridor. His mind was racing *'Apartment 7 Apartment 7, Apartment 7!'*. He nearly slipped over again as he finally reached the door, but he recovered and propped himself against the wall to the right of the entrance. Gun in hand Al was ready to swing round and burst through the door. Then without warning

BANG! BANG! BANG!

A ray of light burst through the apartment door; through a hole made by a bullet that had missed him by less than a foot. *'God'* he thought *'I'm too late'*. He paused then shouted,

"Police!"

Then again

"Police come out with your hands up!"

No response, he reached across and tried the handle, it was open. He turned it very slowly and it swung open. He caught just a hint of cordite in the air as he spa from left to right, gun pointing into the room, but what he saw left him speechless.

The Apartment - Downtown - three minutes earlier.

It was as if time had almost stopped. Not fully as the clocks were still turning but at a quarter of their previous speed. In the same way when you have an accident in a car everyone says the actual crash seems to go on forever, even if it was merely a matter of seconds or even less. For you, in the middle of that crash, it seems like an eternity. Your animal instincts kick in and every one of your senses becomes hyper-sensitive; hearing, eyesight, smell, touch even the supposed sixth sense; your third eye. It all becomes heightened, probably in the same way we hunted for game out on the savanna thousands of years ago. All but forgotten in the modern world, all but forgotten except for those who make their living by hunting their prey.

The Spaniard was sitting in a wooden chair by the window, despite the heat he'd put his thin sports jacket back on. There was a slight gust of wind coming through from outside, just enough to cause a chill. His rifle was cradled in his hands, placed on the tripod atop a small wooden table right by the open window. His view through the scope gave him a laser sharp view through to the restaurant, across the tables outside and inside. Wherever his target sat he'd have him in his sights. He turned briefly to Harris who smiled back and light another cigarette. As he turned away, he thought he caught a movement in the building opposite; maybe the opening or shutting of blinds but after a few seconds of careful observation he dismissed it as the changing sun catching the glass of the window opposite from a different angle. He wasn't stupid he knew he was firing on all cylinders, and his super sensitivity made him susceptible to everything around him.

He began to scan the restaurants al fresco tables; partly to kill time before the target arrived but also to ensure there was nothing out of the ordinary. No large looking gentlemen in black sunglasses, no groups of men looking around with bulges under their armpits, nothing that looked out of place. The attractive Latina lady he'd seen earlier in the sunglasses and large hat had thankfully moved on. He had no wish to upset civilians with the wet work he was about to carry out today.

A young couple sat together towards the front entrance and two older men, grey hair and grey suits, sat together chatting over wine and two large bowls of pasta. They looked very ordinary, probably two local businessmen having lunch catching up, maybe they'd extend it into the afternoon, more wine and a few hits of the hard stuff before commuting home to their families. He understood that you worked your fingers to the bone every day; Friday you often needed to let off a little steam, kick back. Although he found it strange how his own Friday afternoon decompression would involve assassination.

So, it seemed to be a relatively quiet lunchtime at La Romana. Then the large black sedan arrived directly outside, six men dressed in black got out; four bosses and two heavily built bodyguards he noted. They made their way to the front entrance beneath the red plastic awning, the maître d' tried to usher them in. The Spaniard got ready to take his shot.

Then the smallest man in sunglasses and a dark fedora shook his head and pointed to two shaded tables in front of the building. As they sat down the small man removed his hat and lit a cigarette, or rather he had it lit for him by one of the goons.

As the man smoothed down his thinning hair there was a flash of recognition in the Spaniard's mind. He looked again through the scope at the small brown Latin man in the black suit and was convinced this man wasn't an Italian mobster. There was another thought that ran through his mind, a vague awareness of how he'd seen this man before. Who the fuck was this man; how did he know him? He racked his brains. Suddenly he saw this man's face in a newspaper in a bar. This this wasn't a gangster this was something else, this was political.

His train of thought was broken by the smell of Harris - stale beer, sweat and cheap cigarettes - as he lent in towards him.

"That small man to the left, that's your target." said Harris.

"Copy that."

Harris was stood next to him and was looking through a small pair of field glasses.

"Yeah, the little Spic, I mean Wop, towards the front door, you see him?"

The Spaniard looked towards at Harris then back through the scope. The man outside the restaurant was laughing and chatting to his colleagues. Then suddenly a brilliant flash of memory, from a backwater LA cantina, full of beer and working stiffs, a drink with his taxi driver (who he now knew as Jesus from the CIA), then the Russian Colonel made an appearance, then, then. He saw the target's face not in the photograph he'd been given by Bradley and the FEDS but in a newspaper, a Spanish speaking one, called the Opinion or something. The man he was looking at wasn't Italian he was a Nicaraguan.

Fuck, it suddenly dawned on him this wasn't a hit on the mob from here in Los Angeles it was a political assassination. He was looking at the Latin American JFK and he was sat up here in the schoolbook depository playing frigging 'patsy'.

"Take the shot, take it." Harris snarled into his ear.

The Spaniard looked through the site.

"What the Wop? Do you mean the Spic if we're going to be accurate with ethnic slurs?"

He slowly turned his head towards Harris, his right hand leaving the trigger of the gun.

"Take the shot you fuckin' dago prick!"

Harris was pointing a jet-black snub-nosed Smith and Wesson .38 right into his face.

"This isn't a mobster is it Harris?"

"Take the shot motherfucker before I destroy your face!"

There were veins bulging on Harris' neck.

"OK, I'll do it."

He began to turn back towards the prone rifle when suddenly an explosion ripped out the back of the Spaniard's jacket. Harris stumbled backwards looking horrified and shocked. Blood began to spread over his chest, through his dirty white shirt. The Spaniard span round brandishing, the illegal, Walter PP .32

automatic he'd purchased in South Central. It'd been hidden away in the inside pocket of his jacket, where now there was a gaping black smoking hole.

He stepped forward and fired again BANG into Harris chest. The man fell back shocked and tried in vain to raise his gun in response. The Spaniard aimed the Walter at the eye; BANG he shot, putting a bullet straight through the hillbilly's right cheek. A large splash of blood, like a Pollack masterpiece, sprayed across the front door. Harris slid to the floor, dead.

The door creaked open and a wide-eyed sweating Al, swung in brandishing his own pistol. The Spaniard slowly raised his hands and the gun towards the ceiling. He smiled,

"Better late than never old boy, better late than never."

Los Angeles, Santa Monica Freeway

They were back inside the Al's silver shark motoring along the I-10 towards Culver City. Both men were smiling but not through sense of contentment, it was mixture of relief and exhaustion. Al was wiping sweat from his forehead and furiously smoking, whilst the Spaniard stared out of the window letting the breeze from the open window cool and calm him. He needed to be calm and relaxed for the next part of his mission. It was past midday, and the heat had become oppressive but at 60mph with the windows open it was better than aircon.

They'd hightailed it out of the apartment almost immediately after the failed hit. The shooter had wiped down all the surfaces, the gun and picked up the spent cartridges. He'd then placed the rifle in the hands of Harris, ensuring some good fingerprints, and left it on the floor. To LAPD forensics it would look as if the ex-USMC sniper was now the shooter not him. That didn't quite explain Harris' death, the lack of a murderer or of a murder weapon but it was the best he could do. He hoped it'd look like an inside job gone wrong, which in a sense it was.

As he was wiping down the rifle, he glanced across at the building opposite him and noticed a blind had been raised. He saw a tall man with a short blonde haircut moving across the window. He then glimpsed a rifle in his hands. The man looked directly at him, smiled and nodded. Fuck me, he thought, it was one of Colonel Dimitry's goon's who'd cornered him out near China Cove and the one who'd sapped him on the back of the head, he had to stop that happening so often. He figured that the man was there to prevent him shooting this Nicaraguan politician who was probably a Soviet ally. You didn't have much of a choice south of the border it was either the Red Menace or Uncle Sam if you wanted your country to survive.

He looked across at the restaurant below; it was deserted. The Nicaraguans had packed up and shipped out in their big black sedan and the rest of the clientele had either hit the highway or hightailed it inside. When they had done a quick sweep of the room they slowly walked, not run (as not to attract attention) downstairs and into Al's car.

"Al, you left the car running. It could've been stolen."

"I was worried about you amigo."

"Good, now can we go and rescue the girl."

Al laughed; more gallows humour.

"Si Señor!"

Al reversed from the rear of the building into the back alley and then drove out onto the street.

"Hey, how the hell did you find me?"

"I was tailing you and then I lost you."

"I saw, but how did you find the location of the hit?"

"Overton."

"Who?"

"The night porter at your hotel. I saw an older cop when I was searching for you and thought of Overton. You left the address of the hit at the hotel."

"Jesus, that was fortuitus."

"Fortuitus, you fucking Limeys … *fortuitus*. I'll say it was mother-fucking fortuitus"

Both men broke into laughter then silence, they were both emotionally and physically drained. They passed over the 258 - cruising through the lights at sixty - between Jefferson and Arlington Heights. The buildings got slightly smaller as they left Downtown but still it was all concrete jungle, sunshine and palm trees. The Spaniard had put his polarised sunglasses on and was trying to light the remains of this mornings' Cuesta-Rey cigar, the end was frayed, blackened and only a couple of inches long but after a few puffs the cigar fired up like an old classic car: lots of smoke and sparks. He blew a mouthful of smoke towards a VW bug that was crammed full of West Coast blondes, both male and female. The irony that your image of the Californian was that of the bronzed Aryan god; when most of the population were small, brown natives. It reminded him of serving in the dying days of the British Empire; just a few officers from the finest schools in England in charge of the entire world well, a fifth of it at least.

The car hit a rumble strip, and he was jolted back to the here and now. He looked at Al.

"Do you know where Bradley's keeping her?"

"Yep, it's a safe house in Carlson Park, hopefully he won't have gotten word yet that the operation is a bust. We're thirty minutes away."

"Step on it I want this bastard dead."

"I'd warn you that he's still an officer of the law, but I don't think that's gonna have much of an influence on you."

"Al, I've been putting bullets into people for twenty-five years. His rank is the least thing on my mind"

He didn't tell the black PI but the only thing that was on his mind was the safety of Maylin. The thought of her in danger chilled him to the bone.

FBI Safe House - Carlson Park - LA

The fat FED stood in the garden looking at the remains of the once glorious Ballona Creek. Through the chain link fence, he could see a dirty stretch of river - more like a ditch - then a high bank of grey concrete that backed onto the Inglewood Oil Field. He had no idea that less than a hundred years earlier it was an active river. Watercress grew, in abundance, local native American tribes used it was a waterway to gain access to the Pacific and the first Spanish settlers helped themselves to its fragrant waters to irrigate their crops. Now it was merely another storm drain for LA. Like his own life it'd started full of potential and promise and now was just a dried-out husk servicing the greater good.

He'd been a good cop once, a good soldier, he could follow orders. He'd fought in WW2, he'd cleared up local and national crimes as both a beat cop then a FED. Jack Bradley's problem was that he listened to the wrong people and, not being one for caution, had disregarded the right people. This is how he'd come up working indirectly for Hoover, chasing down reds, executing terrorists both foreign and domestic. Getting it all done quickly and at as low a cost as possible.

He smoked his cigarette to the end and tossed it into the once great waterway. Exhaling deeply, he kicked away the rubbish from his feet as he walked through the overgrown lawn of the safehouse.

"Someone should really cut this."

He spoke to no one in particular, as he walked to the backdoor. He was eager to find out if the operation had been a success. He was keen to report the good news to his superiors and take some time off. Maybe go back to Langley, Virginia to see his ex-wife and the kids; more likely a long week down in Tijuana with every conceivable vice that was available to the middle-aged American with a pocket full of cash. He pushed open the screen door and walked into the kitchen.

"Hey, we heard from Harris yet?"

A young thin man in white shirt, black tie and slacks (almost the regulation uniform of the FBI) was sat in the kitchen drinking coffee and smoking.

"No Sir, nothing."

Bradley checked his watch it was a few minutes after one thirty and Harris was supposed to call, from a payphone, telling them the job was a success. Maybe he was on the road, on his way back with good news. He hoped this was the case.

"How's the girl?"

"She's awake sir."

"Does she need another dose?"

Bradley was referring to the injection of sodium pentothal they'd given her when they arrived at the safehouse.

"It'd should've warn off by now, but she still seems pretty much sedated. She's compliant Sir."

"OK I'm gonna hit the head then I want to move this operation to another local. It's been too long, and Harris should've called by now."

"Yes Sir."

The young man with the sharp hair and the creased trousers almost saluted, he was still defined by his training. He'd only been with the agency for twelve months; one tour of 'Nam was enough to convince him he liked serving his country but at slightly less risk and under slightly better conditions. Twelve hours lying in a rice paddy in monsoon season will do that to a man. He heard the toilet flush.

Carlson Park - LA

The silver shark screeched around the corner and headed down a dead-end street; a few single-story houses were at the end. They'd spent precious minutes trying to find the right road. Luckily Al had been given the address of the safehouse by Bradley a few days before, as a rendezvous location if things got hairy.

The problem with LA was that it all looked like much of a muchness. Rapid expansion in the 1940s and 50s meant lots of housing had been thrown up as quickly as possible to meet demand. Everyone wanted a two-bed, two-bathroom single story with a yard outback and a driveway at the front. Ergo Lakeland Avenue looked remarkably like Seafront Road; although the likelihood was neither was by the lake or the sea.

Al suddenly pointed to a weathered bungalow.

"That's it, let's hope she's there!"

The Spaniard took out his Walter and checked it was fully loaded, and the safety was off. They pulled the Chevy up to the curb and both men jumped out racing towards the building. They would be applying no departmental procedure here from any known enforcement agency, if they saw someone, they would be asking questions later and shooting first. They made their way up to the house, sidearms drawn, each creeping up the respective sides of the driveway. Three doors up an older man in a dirty undershirt came out with two bags of trash. On seeing the armed men, he reversed quickly back inside his home.

Al tried the door as the Spaniard peaked through the windows; silent nothing. The door was open, and they silently crept inside, not announcing their presence. They were way beyond that; anyone in this house - apart from the girl - FED, Narc or Spook was a dead man. They both knew this; they'd come too far now.

They crept into an untidy lounge; newspapers were on the floor, ashtrays overflowed with butts and smoke still hung in the air. The kitchen was just as messy. Al made his way towards the back door, and into the garage; nothing. Meanwhile the Spaniard checked the bedrooms. They met back in the lounge, knowing it was a bust.

"Fuck, they're gone." Al said kicking some trash on the floor.

The former Royal Marine remained silent. Al tried to grab his attention.

"Man, I said they're gone, they've blown town."

The Spaniard holstered his weapon and pinched the bridge of his nose.

"Are you listening? I said they're gone, and you've got nothing to say?"

"I understand what you're saying. Clear as a bell, crystal clear but I'm trying to think."

"About what?"

"Someone, anyone, who may know where they are."

Hondo Canyon - LA

Overton couldn't sleep. It was just after two in the afternoon, despite the fact he'd worked an overnight shift and hasn't gone to bed until ten in the morning he was wide awake again. He put it down to age; he was at the later end of his sixties and just didn't need the sleep he'd required forty or even ten years ago, but this was compounded by the fact he often fell asleep at work most nights. It was a relatively easy job, safer than guarding a warehouse, and he had fun socializing with the clientele. This comprised of businessmen, people on holiday and he always had coffee on for the beat cops who he liked to chat with. Yes, he got to meet some interesting people.

Like that British fella who told him to pass on the note to that colored cop, the ex-Marine. As a rule, he didn't care for colored people, twenty-five years working homicide in South Central LA will do that to a man, but this private eye wasn't just a gimpy Leroy, nope he was a goddam Marine and in Overton's book that was better than a letter of recommendation from the Almighty himself.

So, he'd taken the message from the Brit and left it for the day clerk. He had a feeling about certain people; he got a good feeling about those two, he didn't know why he just thought that they were trying to do some good. But he could be wrong, he'd been wrong before and folks had died.

He looked out of his back window, a clear view across the treetops of the Canyon. He could see his large backyard, chicken coops, the small barn behind his house and his slightly down at heal 1951 Studebaker Champion, which was now a weathered grey. He loved that car; still worked with almost 160,000 miles on the clock. He retired with his wife to Santa Monica but after she passed away, he decided to head up into the mountains for a quieter life. No tourists, no crime, no hustle no bustle. It was all trees, retirees and a few hippies and beatniks or whatever they called themselves these days. But they weren't giving him any crap, they just had parties and took drugs. No different to the jazz hopheads back when he still walked the beat with his Colt Official Police '38 (a gun he still owned and was a dead shot with). Also, the LAPD has jurisdiction round here and being an old cop, they looked after their own.

He washed up his cup and plate, leaving them on the drainer he headed out to the front porch. Overton slowly placed himself in the old pine chair by the front door where he had a good view across the hills and down the road. It gave him an almost hidden view of the rest of the countryside as he sat behind one of the large uprights supporting the roof of the porch. Good way to take in the wildlife without disturbing them. He took a battered cigarette from a packet in his shirt pocket and placed it in his mouth. Then with one deft movement, perfected over decades of smoking, he pulled a match out, red with a grey tip, and flicked the end with his thumb. All of this with one hand and in less than a second. It burst into flame, and he gently cupped it bringing it to his mouth and lighting the cigarette. A deep inhale and then exhale, he pulled a thread of loose tobacco from his mouth, no filters for him thank you. He'd been smoking filter-less Luckies since before the war.

All was peaceful, he leaned back into his chair, he could see the sunlight glinting through the trees picking up the ghostly smoke trail of his cigarette. A distant hammer was pounding but very faintly; he guessed it was his neighbor down the road. Like him an old guy who loved to work on his old car in his old shed. Then everything began to slow down, Overton's breathing got heavier, his hand holding the cigarette dropped off the arm of the chair and he began to nod off to sleep.

He was awoken by the screech of tires and the revving of an engine right in front of his house, he sat upright and peered out from behind the pillar. Two men driving a blue 1968 Ford Fairlane has stopped out on the road just opposite his driveway. The fat one in the light blue sports jacket got out of the driver' seat and marched round the front. His companion, a much younger man in a dark suit exited the car with a map in his hand. They placed he map on the hood of the car. He could hear them arguing, but he couldn't be seen from the darkness of the porch and the position of the pillar.

"Are you sure this is the road?"

"Yes sir, I have been here before, it's just over this hill."

"Alright then, let's get there for Christ's sake, this is turning into a fucking disaster."

The men got back into the car and drove off in a plume of blue smog. It seemed to contradict the quiet bucolic nature of the woodland and the hills. Overton picked himself out of his chair and walked out onto the road. He saw the car disappear over the horizon. But he knew where they were going; the road ran out less than a mile down this track and apart from him and his noisy neighbour with the hammer there was only one other property. A house he knew had been empty for an age. He would later say to himself, what a strange coincidence to see these men in this car, for them to stop and argue, for them to reveal where they were headed. But as a cop of more than thirty years on the streets of Los Angeles he knew coincidences did happen. For it is on such chance events that the world turns.

Ocean Hotel- Santa Monica Los Angeles

They drove the silver shark along Ocean drive pulling up outside the faded pink-grey building. Al switched off the engine and they both sat in silence; exhausted. It was almost three o'clock and they had no idea where Maylin, Bradley and his FBI goons were. Al had a pretty good idea that the ratty looking one who'd been shot up downtown by the Spaniard was currently on a mortuary gurney waiting to be cut up; at least he hoped that was the case.

The Spaniard exhaled deeply

"Come on, I need to make a phone call to London."

"OK" replied the tired looking PI.

Al lit a cigarette in the car and got out following the Brit into the reception area of the hotel. He made for the stairs when the desk clerk caught his attention. He was the soft bald non-descript guy who seemed to be the antithesis of the old haggard ex-cop who manned the helm each evening.

"Err excuse me gentlemen I have a message for you from Overton."

Al and the Spaniard looked at each other, a glimmer of hope in both sets of eyes. This was misconstrued as unrecognition by the desk clerk. He qualified the statement.

"He is our night porter."

He handed the Spaniard a piece of paper which read…

Come to my home in Hondo Canyon, that midwestern big fella who looks like a cop is up here with another fella who also looks like a cop. Thought you'd like to know

Overton's address was on the note, the LA ex-street cop had come through for them again.

Just as Al was about to sing the man's praises four uniformed LAPD burst into the lobby brandishing K38 S&W revolvers. The older cop leading the charge pointed a huge Colt Python at them.

"Hands up, you're both under arrest."

The desk clerk behind the counter shrank into the shadows. Al stepped up, all smiles.

"Gentlemen my name is Albert Rogers I'm a Special Assistant with the CIA here in Los Angeles. Can I have your permission to show you, my identification."

The older cop, who was in his early forties, looked flustered and relaxed the grip on his gun. He glanced at each of the two men.

"OK slowly now no funny stuff."

Al put his hand into his jacket and pulled out a black wallet and handed it over to the sergeant.

"This man with me is under my supervision. He is a British subject with diplomatic immunity. I am trying to get him to the safety of our offices downtown. This is a matter of national security."

Al was winging it; he had no idea who'd sent these flatfoots. The Feds, the Agency, or even if they were the real deal. The cop holstered his gun and waved at his men to do the same as he handed back the ID card,

"OK men lower your weapons. This seems to be a non-threatening situation. I'm gonna need to call this in. We're still going to need you to accompany us to the station house."

"That's fine officer, I understand totally, I used to work for the Sherriff's Department in South Central."

"Tough break."

"You're not kidding"

Suddenly another three men in suits burst into the hotel lobby; it was getting crowded. A tall bald man in a blue suit stepped forward brandishing another ID.

"Thomas, FBI I want these two in hand cuffs. Right now."

The older cop looked confused he glanced between Al and the Spaniard and the new group who'd just entered. He looked at the new ID card and stepped up between Al and the Feds. Addressing Thomas he raised his hands.

"OK, OK back down a little pal. Now I suggest we take a trip downtown, and we can figure this all out."

There was the creak of a door followed by a bang as it swung shut.

"You fucking idiot he's got away,"

The bald FBI man pointed towards an empty doorway which was still swinging on its hinges. Al was smiling from ear to ear and the Spaniard was nowhere to be seen.

Pacific Coast - six hours before SoCal rocked

The air was blowing in his hair, and he was tapping on the bottom of the doorframe as he drove the old Nash station wagon out of Los Angles on PCH and towards the Santa Monica Mountains. No music, just the sound of the wind and the rumble of the car. The Americans had only been here for just over a century and the Spanish for another fifty years over that; the original inhabitants had been on this land for more than three and a half thousand years. There was very little left of their people or their culture.

He lit a small bent cheroot that he retrieved from his jacket. He'd bought a packet at the tobacconist back in LA, hand rolled Dominican cigars. They tasted of pepper and liquorish but were very oily, strong and smooth. He exhaled, mentally making a note to cut back on his consumption. Although if there was ever a time to smoke tobacco now was probably it.

The car motored on along PCH or the California State Route 1 - it was quiet; the right side of rush hour and the sun was still trying to scorch the earth before it disappeared for another day. The old car was holding up well; despite the rust, the filth inside and the odd squeak that came from the bodywork, the suspension or the steering wheel. This old girl still had life left in her and the engine was sounding surprisingly smooth. There was a faint smell of gasoline fumes, but he reckoned all the car needed was a proper service and a tune up. There was a dreamcatcher hanging from the rear-view mirror; he had no idea it was part of native American culture; he just presumed it was some of the hippy crap that belonged to the previous owner. He wasn't averse to the counter-culture movement, in fact he'd adopted the foreign cultures of Britain and then Malaya as he became a soldier, an officer and finally a policeman.

He just saw most of it as nothing more than a fashion trend; hair gets longer, skirts get shorter, this religion over that religion, now we smoke weed and don't drink whisky. It'd be something else next week and he felt it was no different to winds of change blowing this way and that.

Still, he left the dreamcatcher where it was, it helped the car blend into the hippy scene of Southern California. He wasn't going to stand out to local cops in this jalopy. In fact, he was surprised how easy his getaway had been. He'd made his way out through the hotel lobby and into the, now disused, kitchen of the hotel. He'd emerged into the rear parking lot and weaved through the parked cars, some belonging to the local police, and onto the small side street that paralleled Ocean Drive. There, next to a disused garage with a dusty For Sale notice on it, was the Rambler. He'd covered the dash with an old, flattened cardboard box when he'd parked the car there yesterday. It stopped the sun heating up the interior too much and made it look a little abandoned. The keys were still atop of the rear wheel, where he'd left them, and the old girl started up first time. The Spaniard then made his way round the back of the hotel, out onto the Ocean Drive and then onto PCH.

He's stopped off to buy fuel and ask directions at a gas station near Sunset Beach. The attendant came out, fuelled up the car, checked the oil and even washed his windshield. All very novel for a European: back in England you filled up the car yourself and there was nothing in the realm of food or beverages on offer at a gas station. Here he'd bought a couple of very cold cokes and a tin of Planters Cocktail Nuts - he couldn't remember the last time he'd eaten.

The Spaniard tipped the young man a buck as he replaced the fuel cap on the car.

"Excuse me do you know where this address is?"

The young man took the piece of paper and studied it then smiled.

"Sure mister, it's up Hondo Canyon" Handing the piece of paper back to him.

"You gotta head up PCH, then take a right onto Topanga. After a couple of miles or so you'll some to a fork, take the smaller road on the left that's Old Topanga Canyon Road. Hondo Canyon Road is the fourth or fifth turning on the left again. Hey, wait I'll go draw you a map; my uncle lives near there."

The teenager disappeared and came back with a small map drawn on a paper napkin. He was all smiles, freckles and dirty blonde hair. The Spaniard smiled and thanked him offering another dollar for his trouble.

"No mister I can't take that, just you remember to come back here on your way back for gas. And I can give you a good price on a new set of tyres if you like. These old ones have seen better days."

The Spaniard smiled, always upselling the Americans, but hey it was better than the stony-faced mechanics back in Britain.

"Thanks, I'll be back for that gasoline."

As he drove off the young man shouted after him

"…and the tires mister and the tires!"

Hondo Canyon Road

Jack Bradley paced up and down the worn Navajo rug in the front room of the cabin. He had a dark green dial telephone in his left-hand and he was shouting into the receiver in his right.

"Just get me the Chief. I need to know what he's proposing."

He stood and looked skywards for divine intervention, which didn't come.

"Is the British contractor in custody? You're not sure? Jesus will someone get me the Director or Tolson; I need official confirmation on what we're doing now."

Again, he paused and waited for an answer. He turned to Frank, the young thin agent in the black suit who'd driven them up here to the FBI safe house. Bradley signalled for a light as he placed a cigarette between his lips. Frank handed him a cheap metal lighter and walked over to the large window that illuminated the cabin.

"Not available? What do you mean not available I'm our here on my fucking ass trying to … hello, hello?"

He smashed the receiver into the phone's cradle.

"They hung up. Can you believe that they hung up on me? Jesus, I need to speak to the Director, this is who we're working for. He's gotta take the ball on this thing."

Frank turned around and looked at Bradley. He picked up his lighter, that Bradley had discarded on the table-top, and lit his own cigarette. He smoked Galois - he'd acquired a taste for them in Saigon. He'd also developed an ability for instinct whilst serving his tour in Vietnam. It'd kept him alive more than once. Currently his inner monologue was screaming - *get the fuck out of there … now!*

Frank looked towards the open door of the cabin's only bedroom. There tied to the bed was a furious looking Latina with jet black hair. The gag in her mouth was the only reason they couldn't hear her swearing in guttural Spanish. Her legs were kicking out and obviously the mickey they'd dosed her with had worn off.

Frank lent against the frame of the bedroom door. She reminded him of his last time on R&R in Saigon. A pretty young Vietnamese girl who he'd picked up at a bar convinced him to go back to her room. He wasn't naïve, he knew she was a prostitute, but she kept playing pop and rock records in her room and before he knew it was dawn. He didn't care they hadn't made love; he'd had too much fun talking and dancing, drinking and smoking weed with this beautiful young girl. It felt normal, like back at home and not out in the field, killing and being killed.

They eventually copulated, as per the contract, just after the sun came up. He didn't really remember that, but he could never forget her kicking her legs on the bed and shaking her long jet black her to Tommy James and The Shondells.

"Frank, hey Frank are you with us?"

He straightened up and turned back to Bradley who was drinking a bottle of beer and smiling.

"Yes sir. Sorry I was just checking on the girl."

"Looked a lot more than checking to me. Hey, you may even get to have a little fun with her before the day is out."

Bradley laughed coarsely, looking towards Maylin, before he inhaled deeply from his cigarette

"Err no sir that's not really part of the operation. It would be unprofessional."

"Son with all due respect this whole thing ain't procedural. We went off the reservation a long time ago and I'm gonna have to use all my wiles to get us outta this shit creek. But you're with me, right?"

"Of course, sir, one hundred percent."

"That's, what I thought." Said Bradley as he blew smoke skywards.

Frank's brain was screaming, how the hell did he get here. This job was supposed to be legit, signed off by Hoover, green lit by the government. Now it looked like they were all being hung out to dry. First chance, he thought, first chance I get, and I am out of here. Back to LA then hop on a silver bird and fly off to Quantico ASAP.

"Shall I make us some coffee sir?"

"Sounds like a plan Frank."

Frank went to the kitchen and began to mentally make a note of how he was going to get the fuck out of Dodge.

Overton's Place - 20th Century California

He took the second left turn onto Hondo Canyon Road; it was an asphalt surface but only just and it was narrow. Thankfully he didn't meet any traffic coming the other way and figured this was probably a pretty isolated location. The Rambler was still going strong, and he glanced down at the napkin given to him by the young man back at the gas station. It read 'only about two or three houses down this road'. OK better check on the first I see, he thought. As he pulled into the wide driveway an old man walked out of the front door and waved to him. It was Overton. He walked down the porch steps and towards the station wagon. As the Spaniard got out of the car the former policeman stepped back as if assessing the road worthiness of the car and the measure of the driver.

"I'm surprised that old thing managed to make it all the way up here."

"Hey back in England this thing is virtually brand new."

"Things that bad over there?"

"Well, we still owe America millions of dollars for funding World War Two."

"Hell, well as they say you can't avoid death and taxes."

The two men shook hands, and the Spaniard got straight to the point.

"Where's Bradley and the other Fed?"

"Hold your horses Honcho, come into the house and I'll explain."

"I'd really like to just know where they are?"

"Son I'm nearly seventy years of age. Now if you want me to help you, we're gonna need a plan. I know they got at least two guys down there who're young and ready for action. Let's just make sure we're one step ahead of them."

As they walked out onto the rear porch Overton explained what he'd seen that afternoon. Convinced it was the same fat man who'd visited the Spaniard at the hotel who'd also stopped outside. The Spaniard explained they had Maylin (probably stowed in the trunk) and that they had been setting him up to execute a South American politician as part of an FBI operation.

"Sweet Baby Jesus. OK I now understand why you're eager to get over there. Shoot, I knew they killed JFK I just thought that was the exception to the rule and not the rule. Guess I was wrong."

"I was contracted to do the job; I thought for the US government. Then I find out it's not quite for them but a rogue branch of the FEDS and it's not an organised crime boss that I'm shooting but a foreign politician."

"Well, I see the corruption hasn't changed much since I was walking the beat during Prohibition."

The view from the rear porch was stunning, you could see clear across the valley. It was arid but the Spring rain had caused many of the cacti to bloom and the sky was a clear and blue. It reminded him of Andalucía in Southern Spain.

Overton pointed out his neighbour's blue house a mile or so away and then said there was one more property on the road. He thought it'd been empty for some time, maybe a holiday retreat for someone in the hills. It was the only place they could be holed up. Overton picked up his police service revolver from the kitchen table and wiped it with an old rag. A box of new shells was sat unopened.

"Why are you helping me?" asked the Spaniard.

"Well seems like the right thing to do son. You seem like a good man and well if I'm honest I'm bored out of my mind up here. I could do with a little action."

Both men laughed,

"You gotta piece?"

The Spaniard showed him his small black Walter

"That'll do. We better get hunting."

Santa Monica Police Department

The two men sat side by side inside the interview room of the local police station. The older of the men, an Hispanic gentleman with dark hair that was greying at the sides, was drinking a cup of coffee and staring into space. The younger, a black man in his late thirties, was smoking a cigarette and starring intensely at the cheap metal ashtray that was on a bolted down table. He would occasionally flick ash in the direction of the ashtray; unconcerned over whether it would hit its mark or not. Both men had had their ties removed, as was procedure when holding someone for questioning in California.

The door to the room opened and a group of men entered. The Latino male straightened up but his counterpart just continued to stare at the ashtray in front of him. He flicked some more ash; it landed nowhere near the ashtray.

"Lawyer … now." said the black man.

"Al shut up it's the Director." Responded the Latino

"Fuck your Director I want legal representation, and I want it…"

Al looked up and was firstly shocked to see a group of at least ten people standing in front of him. A few seriously high-up cops - the brass wearing the full regalia and the rest obviously plain clothes but with an air of seniority. The group parted like the red sea and a small elderly man with a stout frame, beady eyes and slicked back dyed hair stepped forward.

"Gentlemen I'm sure we don't need to involve any outside agencies in this. I am convinced we can overcome this little impasse. For the good of both our agencies and that of the country as a whole."

Al stubbed out his cigarette and straightened up. He was looking at a man who's picture he'd seen on TV and newspapers hundreds of times since he was a kid, one of the men who'd inspired him to become a policeman and a living legend who had run the Federal Bureau of Investigation for the best part of half a century.

Al whispered to Jesus,

"Hey, it that who I think it is?"

Jesus whispered back in Spanish.

"Si es El Jefe."

The small man pulled up a seat and sat down. An assistant to his left did the same and took out a notebook and pen.

"Now gentlemen it would appear as if we have a rogue elements within my agency that have been greenlighting covert operations that go against the aims and regulations of my agency. Thankfully our friends within the CIA."

He looked at Jesus

"…and their contractors."

He looked at Al

"Have brought this issue to light and I, for one, am most grateful for the work that this agency, who usually specialise in areas outside this country of ours, have carried out on our behalf to bring to an end the misdeeds of these people from within my organisation."

Jesus raised his finger to says something but a large man in dark glasses, who stood behind the small man seated at the table, just shook his head gently from side to side. Jesus put his arm down. The small man continued.

"This being said I, can see that there would be no positive gain from making these incidents public as they would only weaken the strength of both our organisations and place the country, as a whole, in a far more precarious situation both internally and externally.'"

He coughed into his hand and continued,

"I therefore would request that both you men sign a document to ensure this incident and all incidents surrounding it are kept away from the public eye; as to preserve the work of fellow countrymen in their pursuit of justice in this great nation of ours."

The small man rose from the table shook the hands of both men seated and left the room. Another large man in a dark blue suit and black sunglasses placed two copies of what looked like legal documents in front of them.

"Gentlemen please sign these."

Al looked in amazement at Jesus and Jesus grabbed the papers and began to sign them.

"Jesus did we just get told to shut the fuck up by J Edgar Hoover?"

"Yep."

Hondo Canyon - California

He was running through the brush and trying not to fall into the canyon as he made his way on foot back to the main road, the 27, and from there he figured he could hitch a ride to PCH and onto LAX. He'd tried to take the car, but Bradley was twirling the keys on his finger as he spoke to someone at the LA Office. They were being very unhelpful, and Frank figured that this operation was a bust and it was time to hit the road before it got aborted. He was worried that in the clean-up he'd get aborted too.

Frank made his way over a series of rocks and more brush before coming to a halt in a small clearing. He was covered in dust and dirt; the Californian Hills were dry for most of the year with wildfires being quite an issue. He sat on one of the rocks just to catch his breath and wipe the sweat out of his eyes. The FBI agent had been recruited directly by Bradley for this gig about a month ago. He'd just returned from a sting operation in Miami involving a local drug kingpin and after a few weeks at Quantico he was eager to get back into the field. Bradley told Frank at first it was a very hush hush operation answering only to the very top. He'd met that black PI and then that ex-Marine Harris and worked out that this whole thing was a black op. He realised that if things went south the Bureau could genuinely say it knew nothing.

Frank wiped the sweat from his face with a once clean handkerchief and checked his gun. The Colt'38 with the long six-inch barrel was still under his armpit in a black leather holster. He pulled the weapon out checked it was in good condition, wiped it and reholstered it. He knew the gun was there, but it felt better to physically check the piece. Once in the military, always in the military.

He caught a glimpse of something on the horizon. It was the windscreen of a car glinting in the sun. He saw the blacktop of the road and figured he'd walked down to the 27 from the upper part of the valley. He dusted himself down and moved at a steady pace down towards the highway; time to flash his ID and commandeer a vehicle to get back to civilization; well Los Angeles at least. To be honest he hated the West Coast he hated the smog, the heat, the laid-back hippy attitude that even the old timers seemed to have. In his mind it was as if the state of California belonged to Mexico as the locals all had an easy-going attitude to everything. It was all 'Mañana, Mañana.' Even the rednecks and hill billies back in Virginia were more together than these assholes. God, he hoped for a posting on the East Coast next time; New York, Boston, either would do, just not near these flaky losers.

He reached the blacktop just as a car rounded the bend and headed towards him - it was a large black Chevy sedan with two men in the front. Frank dusted himself off and straightened his tie, pulling out his FBI badge and raised his hand in the air to stop the vehicle. The car came to a stop a few feet from where he stood; he moved to the front passenger window giving the universal 'wind down' signal of an index finger in a circular motion. The passenger complied.

"Hello gentlemen, my name's Frank Osbourne I'm with the FBI and I need to commandeer this vehicle to take me back into Los Angeles."

The two blond men in the front of the car just looked at him stone faced, unsmiling and strangely as if not understanding him.

"OK fellas let's not make this hard…"

"We cannot help you officer."

A deep foreign voice echoed from the rear of the car.

"Dis is a diplomatic car and we are not subject…"

"Sir this isn't a matter of asking; this is a matter of ordering. Now I'm requesting you folks get out of the vehicle as part of my operation here in…"

"No cannot, this car is property of foreign government in your country and as such is not part of the United States of America jurisdiction."

Frank was starting to get angry, who the fuck was this asshole with the foreign sounding voice in the back of the car giving him orders. He unbuttoned his holster and took out his gun addressing the man to the rear of the car. A man obscured by tinted privacy glass.

"I won't tell you again sir. Please can you and your passengers…"

Unfortunately for Frank Osbourne this was definitely a case of being in the wrong place at the wrong time. He didn't get to the next part of the sentence or hear the three loud cracks. A suppressed pistol had fired at point blank range from the front passenger seat. It was a low velocity silenced gun and Frank was dead before he collapsed into a heap on the road a hole to his head and two in his chest.

The rear window wound down and Colonel Dimitry peered out at the now dead FBI agent. In Russian he spoke to his two men.

"This American must be one of those with the Nicaraguan girl, we must be near their safe house. Get rid of this and let's keep looking."

The two suited Russian heavies exited the front of the car, checked and stripped the agent of both his gun and ID and dumped the body into the ravine alongside the highway. It would lie there for the next decade eventually discovered as a John Doe.

Hondo Canyon Road

Overton and the Spaniard approached the neighbouring property from the side. They'd walked up most of the road and decided that for the last 200 yards it'd be better to creep up on the safe house from an unseen vantage point. They'd passed Overton's neighbour, the blue house, and cut into the woods coming up behind the next property via the tree line.

The brush wasn't that thick; the dry Californian wind and sun making it an easy place to trek through. Try this in the jungles of SE Asia, mused the Spaniard, and you'd end up hopelessly lost; consumed by the forest flora or fauna. Plus, the humidity of the jungle meant your clothes literally rotted off your back. Overton's voice brought him back to their current dilemma.

"Shush - we're here, get down."

Both men ducked behind a group of small boulders and scrub. Ahead they could see the outside of a large wooden cabin. A newish blue Ford Fairlane was parked outside, Bradley's car, but apart from that all was quiet on the Western Front. Overton turned round and crouched on his haunches next to the Spaniard.

"You take the back I'll take the front?"

"Standard American police practice?"

"Standard LAPD practice apart from one thing?"

"And what's that."

"No warrant and I shoot to kill."

"It'll be like being back in the British Army then."

He smiled, patting Overton on the back and signalled for them to move off. The old LA cop headed towards the front porch whilst he made for the back of the property. He followed the tree line hiding behind a particularly large Western Juniper. He slid down its trunk and army crawled to towards one of the side windows. The house was probably getting on for hundred years old and looked weathered, the wooden boards on its side were turning white in the Californian sun. The windowsill was rotten, and paint flaked onto the brown dry grass. The Spaniard rose slowly and tried to look inside the building, but the sunshine blocked his view of the interior. The window was open, he could smell cigarette smoke and cooking. He risked manoeuvring to get a better look inside and caught a glimpse of Bradley making his way towards the front door. He then heard Overton shout,

"Don't move you son-of-a-bitch."

Then a loud bang followed by two more. He made it round the front just in time to see the Blue Ford Fairlane drive off: its rear window a spider's web of shattered glass. Overton was on the floor. He'd been winged by Bradley, a hole in the top of his right shoulder.

"Are you alright?"

"Nope but I'll live. Don't' worry I managed to hit the bastard in the leg - which'll slow him down. He had the girl with him in the front seat."

The Spaniard helped the old LAPD cop to his feet and placed his handkerchief over the wound.

"Fuck - where the hell are they going?"

"I've no idea but I tell you son. Go and get that beat up piece of crap you call a car from outside my place, we'll get to them before they get there."

"How on earth are we going to do that?"

Overton placed a bent cigarette between his lips and lit it. Exhaling smoke he smiled at the Spaniard.

"Like the good old Wild West - we'll cut them off at the pass."

The Canyons of Los Angeles

Bradley was bleeding from the wound in his leg, but it was just a graze and hadn't hit the femoral artery. He pulled the car over and taken off his tie, tying it around his leg to stem the flow. He had no idea who that ancient fucker was who'd burst in on him but he wasn't going to let that ancient bastard take him down.

He was in a bad mood before that old geezer turned up as he realised his second in command; Osborne had disappeared. Bradley assumed that's what he'd done as there was no sign of him at the safehouse. He immediately panicked and decide to move the girl to another location; maybe even just dump her somewhere on the highway and take off.

He'd given the girl another dose of sodium pentothal when he pulled over to the side of the road to stem the wound. She was tied up and couldn't react against having the injection. The last thing he wanted was a hot-headed Latin type trying to kick him in the head as he drove down one of these canyon roads. He lit a cigarette before he pulled back onto the road; checking that he wasn't being followed. He wasn't. The car revved and bucked slightly as it got back onto the blacktop from the dusty side of the highway, but the powerful motor soon eased the car into a steady rhythm as they motored through the Santa Monica Mountains towards the Pacific.

He'd seen that fucking Limey bastard in his rear-view mirror as he motored away from the safehouse. But he knew they were miles away from there now and far enough to know they weren't being chased. He looked down at the girl; she was quiet and still but still alive. She was laid across the bench seat, her hands tied, and her long black hair was draped across her face. It moved gently so he knew she was breathing. He took a hit from the cigarette and winced, the wound in his leg had stopped bleeding but it still hurt like hell.

He blew smoke out of the window and mused; the last time he'd been wounded was 1945; the big push towards Berlin and some old-timer with a Panzerfaust had hit the sided of his jeep near Magdeburg. End of his war and for the old German; he'd made sure of that with his machine gun. Jesus by the end they were just fighting veterans from World War One and kids, literal children some no more than twelve years old. As he reminisced the trauma of war as a twenty-year-old soldier a Studebaker Champion appeared from nowhere and clipped his rear quarter causing the car to almost careen off the road into the canyon.

"Son-of-a-bitch."

He shouted to no one in particular. He corrected the course of the car looking into the rear-view mirror. He could see the old man in the passenger seat and the Limey driving. He cursed again realising they must have used a short cut to get to him.

He pushed hard on the gas towards PCH which he could see coming up ahead; the sun was glinting off the blue, azure Pacific. Without slowing down he turned left into traffic, driving across commuters coming out of LA and causing several angry motorists to shake their fists and beep horns. The Chevy's wheels squealed but he straightened it up and gunned the sedan. He was opening up the distance between him and his pursuers. Less than a mile later the pursuers' luck ran out.

California, PCH, Spring

They were beginning to catch up to the Ford Fairlane, as they drove down the magnificent thoroughfare that is the Pacific Coast Highway. The Spaniard was gunning the engine on the old Nash Rambler when suddenly the car started to shudder and stall, it coughed asthmatically and slowed right down. Then the engine just gave up the will to live and shut down completely. A death rattle came from beneath the hood.

"What the hell?

The old man pointed to a pullout on the side of PCH and the Spaniard pulled in. He smashed his hands on the top of the wheel and swore again. He watched in agony as the blue Ford Fairlane made its way off into the distance. They both exited the car. Overton raised his head, catching a whiff of something and walked round to the rear.

"Smell that?"

"Petrol erm Gasoline"

The Spaniard bent to the ground and touched a small damp patch beneath the car.

"Mierda, puta"

He kicked the rear wheel.

"The petrol tank's leaking, maybe when we hit Bradley's car or something. Mind you it's so old this piece of shit's probably rusted through. We're screwed, we'll never catch them now."

"Let's not get hasty son."

Overton smiled and walked straight out into the on-coming traffic - he was holding up what looked like a police badge, probably his old one, and brandishing his service revolver. A 340 brown and white Plymouth Barracuda slammed on his breaks and squealed to a holt stopping just a few feet from Overton. A large man, all blonde hair and muscles, straight out of Central Casting for surfers leaned out of the car.

"What the fuck are you doing get out of the road you idiot."

Overton calmly walked up to the driver's window

"Police son I'm gonna need to commandeer this vehicle."

The blonde driver in his early thirties was a fine example of muscle-bound SoCal: all tight t-shirt and faded jeans. He took off his sunglasses and smiled.

"You aint commandeering shit old man"

Overton shoved his pistol into the man's face.

"Yes, I am son. I am the law, and you will be giving us this car. Now please get out … sir."

"You're fuckin' crazy."

Now looking shocked the blonde surfer exited the car; the engine was still running. Overton smiled nodded and instructed the Spaniard to get in. The muscleman looked at them both, dumfounded. Overton tipped his non-existent hat.

"The LAPD thanks you son."

"Hey, hey where's my receipt. My fucking proof that you're taking my goddam car. Are you sending someone to pick me up?"

"Goodbye son."

And with that the car speed off in a cloud of dust. Neither the Spaniard nor Overton could hear the man call after them.

"LAPD my fucking ass. Who the fuck are you chasing Al Capone? You old bastard."

The 'Cuda was a beautiful car, and the Spaniard gunned the 340 engine, moving through the gears in a bid to catch to Bradley, and more importantly Maylin.

PCH - Southbound - towards Santa Monica

"Gun this motherfucker."

Overton commanded the Spaniard. He met no resistance from him as the red arm of the speedometer started to turn clockwise towards fifty, then beyond seventy and now it touched eighty-five. Likewise, the tachometer pulsed up towards the red line and then back down every time the driver accelerated and then shifted gear. The car shot forward like a bullet out of a gun. The Spaniard swerved and braked avoiding hitting any other vehicles on the relatively quiet highway.

"Shit I can't see that Ford Fairlane."

He was looking side to side and rising out of the seat to look over the traffic in front.

"Calm down son and go faster. That SOB has got serious mileage on us."

He dragged his good arm through his matted hair.

"OK, OK, we're gonna get them."

The Spaniard nervously smiled

"I sure hope so."

The old LAPD cop was playing his cards close to his chest, and those who really knew him would've said he looked worried.

Another few minutes went by as they sped along the PCH towards Santa Monica. That's where it was going to get sticky as there were several major exits. Miss one of these and the game was up. Bradley and Maylin could disappear into LA, or just head south, and they'd never catch up with them. With this in mind, the Spaniard pressed hard on the gas and the 'Cuda bumped up to ninety. It now seemed as if all the other traffic was travelling through thick honey as the commuters and day trippers plodded along the PCH. If he'd have bothered to look, he'd have seen angry drivers wave their fists or give him disparaging hand gestures as he bobbed and weaved through the traffic. He saw a dark blue station wagon, a black Chevy sedan and a dark green Chrysler Newport but no sign of the Ford.

The clock was ticking on the dash and time seemed to be slowing. The Spaniard was sweating and kept darting his eyes across the landscape of the PCH; all to no avail. He wanted to smoke but now was not the time as his speed crept up to 94mph. He couldn't lose her now, it was just too much, he wouldn't fail her. Images of his wife, dead now almost fifteen years, flashed before his eyes. He saw the car destroyed by Chinese terrorists in Kula Lumpur. He was running towards it, but it was too late. The black Wolseley was engulfed in flames and his wife's lifeless body trapped underneath. A trickle of blood slowly making its way down her stocking; pooling on the asphalt.

"We better find her soon; we're coming up on the ten."

Overton's words brough him back to present day Los Angeles.

"If we don't find her before then we're screwed."

The Spaniard's response was to grunt and press the accelerator harder to the floor. The situation seemed fruitless; if they didn't find the car soon Bradley could either be heading for the centre of LA or heading down to LAX and the south and from there God only knew. Suddenly Overton jumped up in his seat and pointed to the left of the highway.

"Got it, got it, they're heading for the ten."

Just ahead the Spaniard saw the dark blue Ford heading off towards LA and Highway 10, at least he hoped it was the right car. He pulled across four lanes of traffic, causing many to brake and others to hit their horns. A large truck carrying lumber was now in front of him. He needed to be on the other side of this to make the turn off

"Get out of the way you bastard!"

Accelerating the car, he swung in front of the international truck causing it to break. He had no time to look back and see the driver struggle to keep the vehicle from tipping over or the ten foot long wooden two by fours that had fallen off the bed and were now littering the highway. Other drivers were now skidding and swerving to avoid taking out their wheels on the constructional wood. Horns blared and angry Californians leaned out of their car windows shouting expletives.

The old cop and the middle-aged mercenary were all to oblivious to this. All they knew is that they had their target back in their sights about 200 yards ahead of them. The Spaniard whipped his forehead and asked Overton to light him a cigarette.

"I thought you only smoked cigars?"

"In this case I'll make an exception."

The old man laughed and fished two filter less smokes out of his shirt pocket. He light both and placed one into the Spaniard's mouth.

"Yeah, I think you deserve this."

Out on the Freeway - SoCal!

Bradley had no idea the pair chasing him had switched cars. He motored through Santa Monica Beach and got off PCH onto the freeway. Heading north he gunned the car, it was a pretty standard Ford government issue but had the 289 cubic-inch V8 - which was an option, so although this looked like an old man's car - in navy blue - it drove like a scalded cat. What they call a sleeper car he mused to himself. He turned the car off the 10 and got onto the 405. Think, he had to think. The girl began to stir, and he decided it was about time to call this thing in.

Alright, this was a black op. but he was only a pawn or maybe even a knight - whatever the fuck was above the pawn in chess. Sure, he was running this operation, but higher powers were in charge. He knew this thing ran all the way up to the FBI big boss Hoover. Although it was being funded out of a slush fund and certainly well away from Congress, he understood that others could carry the can and that he wasn't going to be indicted as the patsy. Best case scenario they'd pay him off, move him to another department and brush it wall under the carpet. Worse case he'd serve time and loose his pension but at the moment, with blood leaking from the wound in his leg that didn't feel too bad.

He looked across at the drugged up Latino girl. Pretty cute, he'd already coped a feel of her breasts and legs earlier that day. Shame he'd not be able to enjoy this one. Mind you, he thought, plenty more whores in the sea. He decided it was time to pass this problem onto senior management.

The car motored past Belair, Mulholland Drive and Sherman Oaks as he pondered his next move. He picked up the handset underneath the dashboard.

"This is Quebec Sierra One Five, Quebec Sierra one five calling Dispatch, Los Angeles 935 Pennsylvania."

A few moments passed then the radio under the dash crackled into life.

"Dispatch LA 935 Pennsylvania to Quebec Sierra One Five."

"Yes, hello Dispatch I wanna call in some backup. I got a 10-95 and I've got two 10-32s in I think a Rambler tailing my vehicle on the 405 North."

"Confirm two 10-32s following you on the 405 North and you're escorting a 10-95."

"Confirmed."

Bradley had just notified FBI headquarters that he was bringing a suspect in and that he was being tailed by two gunmen and wanted backup.

"Quebec Sierra One Five - we have a four-man team in Sylmar head towards the Five, get onto the five and head north towards the new Newhall Pass; they'll meet you there."

"10-76 to the Newhall Pass on the Five. Confirmed"

"Quebec Sierra One Five - Your team are in a black '68 Belvedere licence 566 MAR. Repeat black sedan licence 566 Mike Alfa Romeo."

Bradley was scribbling the plate number onto the back a packet of cigarettes as he drove. Good, he thought, time for some backup to get me out of this situation. Then what? Well, the boss will want to keep this whole situation quiet and if I'm really lucky maybe a nice easy posting somewhere very quiet and hot like Florida. And if not, well that didn't bear thinking about.

Bradley powered down his window and lit another cigarette, blowing smoke out onto the 405. He was comforted by the rhythmic beat of the tamper lines on the concrete and the sunshine which glinted across the top of the nearby palm trees and warmed his face. Yes, everything was gonna be alright he told himself.

What he couldn't see, even in his rear view, was a brown and white 'Cuda that had been following him since Santa Monica and the two men that were determined to see justice served.

Sylmar - The Valley

The black unmarked Plymouth Belvedere screamed out of the central San Fernando Police Department parking lot. The four FBI agents inside had been meeting with counterparts in the local PD to investigate possible student anarchist and communist activity on the Cal State Northridge Campus. To the agents this looked like penny-ante stuff; certainly, nothing to build a career on. Students had occupied an administration building, they had held a rally, some had been expelled and some arrested. But this certainly wasn't the fall of Western democracy. Just kids being kids. The agents were more than excited with the prospect of taking on a couple of perps chasing a fellow Fed.

The Plymouth's exhaust pipe clipped the road as the car spun into main street traffic and headed towards the five. They were meeting the car at the newly constructed Newhall Pass intersection. It meant they could get their man off the freeway and engage the suspects without the fear of an eighteen-wheeler barrelling down on the crime scene.

The driver turned to the agent in the front seat

"This'll liven up the day."

The agent put on his dark sunglasses and smiled,

"Gotta be better than listening to local cops telling us how they got Commies infiltration the college. Jesus this is the Valley, it ain't Da Nang!"

Raucous laughter broke out in the car. All four of the men had fought in Vietnam, all of them were accomplished officers and all brought their A-game as well as their Colt 45 ACPs and two Remington shotguns. They were ready to take on a battalion if not an army.

Ten minutes before the event - San Fernando Valley

The Spaniard was smoking the last of a small cigar he'd been saving in the inside of his coat pocket. Jesus he'd give his high teeth for a strong black Spanish café sin leche right now. He looked across at Overton, the old man was a little pale but the bleeding in his arm had stopped. Thankfully Bradley's shot had just clipped him and missed the vital arteries.

They were still following Bradley's car from a distance heading towards Santa Clarita. The blue Ford went to turn off towards the Route 14 exit but pulled over to the side of the road behind a black sedan. They were next to an overpass which connected Highway Five to the road to Palmdale. It looked like a new extension to the highway.

The Spaniard slowed down and pulled in ahead of the two parked cars, about 50 yards behind them. He was conscious that this could be an ambush. Overton leaned in and pulled out his gun.

"Looks like we may have some trouble at the pass Hombre."

The Spaniard pulled on the handbrake, turned off the car and sat listening to the car rumble to a halt. The engine made pinking noises as it began to cool down in the hot Californian sun. The landscape was as barren, and the traffic had become very light. There was an eerie stillness as if something was about to happen. The sky was bright blue but clear of clouds and with no sign of birds. It seemed as if the world was paused; awaiting unseen event that was about to happen. In the same way people often talk about an eclipse of the sun. One could understand how the ancients thought the darkness and stillness of totality signified the end of the world. This was the same feeling and the Spaniard's senses were firing on overload. He was ready to spring into action.

Bradley struggled out of the blue Ford and approached the black sedan ahead of him. Then suddenly four men exited the car; all dressed in black suits looking ready to easily take on an elderly cop and this middle-aged mercenary. Overton leaned in towards the Spaniard.

"Looks like he called in the cavalry!"

The Edge of Consciousness … somewhere West of the Pecos

Maylin was happily playing in a field near her grandfather's small homestead. The sun was high in the sky and she, as a young teenage girl on the verge of womanhood, was throwing a ball up in the air and trying to catch it. Sometimes she was lucky, and she clasped the ball to her chest bringing it in like a seasoned outfielder at Fenway Park. Sometimes the midday Nicaraguan sun glinted in her eyes, and she missed the ball, it landed on the baked mud and rolled off into the grass.

And then she was aware of a sound. A rumbling in the distance. She looked across the horizon and could see smoke emanating from Volcan Conception. The ancient volcano began to rumble and the whole sky had turned black.

Light broke through the clouds and there was a ringing in her ears. She bent over and threw up onto her feet and she suddenly released she was no longer in late 1950s Nicaragua but in an early 1970s sedan with a fat Mid-Westerner in a terrible blue sports coat. The Californian sunlight was blinding through the windshield as she slowly regained consciousness. She could see the large face of the man who'd kidnapped and drugged her.

"Ah, you're awake missy, time to earn your keep."

She blacked out again but came round enough to see that she was in front of the car and a bunch of men in black suits were approaching her. She could hear the fat man in the blue sports jacket shouting at them and it seemed the whole world. She couldn't really make sense of what he was saying as she'd been given enough dope to knock out a horse. And at five foot four and just under 110 pounds she really was quite easy to tranquilize with just a small dose.

She was pissed, tired and generally fed up with all the bullshit she'd been through recently and struck out at what looked like a wound on her captor's leg. He screeched and slapped her across the face with the back of his hand. It stung and had the effect that he'd been hopping for; that of making her focus. She could now see the four men in black had their guns out pointed at an old man and a rather attractive Latino man that she was convinced she knew but just couldn't place.

As she mused a hand again slapped her across the face. This made her furiously focused.

"Stand up you bitch."

In a flash she was back in Nicaragua, beneath the mighty Conception being taught by her grandfather summer after summer, how to defend herself. How to ward off attackers and how to shoot a gun. She forced open her eyes and saw the piece dangling in its holster from beneath the fat man's jacket. She shook her head, focused, and reached for the gun.

She was sure she heard a loud bang, then she blacked out. When she awoke the event had happened and it appeared she'd died and been transported to Hieronymus Bosch's artistic impression of hell. Fire from the sky, loud explosions and smoke everywhere.

'Never mind' she mused as one of the underworld's devils carried her off 'it's been a good life.'

Los Angeles 1971 - San Fernando Earthquake.

The devil in question wasn't really from the underworld, despite spending many years in hell. He was just your average Spanish mercenary who was trying to save, a more than capable, Nicaraguan woman from the forces of nature.

As Maylin was pulled out of the car by Bradley, she saw the Spaniard and Overton, being surrounded by a group of men in black suits. The FEDS in the suits were now confused as they'd been called in by fellow Agent Bradley but were now facing these two unknown quantities. One was a retired LAPD officer and the other some Limey who claimed to be working with the CIA. Alarm bells had started to ring with one of the FEDs.

"OK lower your weapons everyone I'm calling this shit in. This is way above my pay grade."

Bradley had pulled a stumbling Maylin from his car,

"Fellas as a Special Agent in Charge I outrank all of you. I'm afraid I'm trying to protect this young lady and get her into protective custody away from these two men. Two men, I might add, who're wanted in connection with the attempted assassination of a Nicaraguan politician downtown earlier today. Now how this lady is involved we don't yet know but I need your help to detain these criminals before…"

Maylin began to wake up from her drugged stupor. She murmured and dribbled,

"Fuuh…You"

She punched Bradley in the bullet wound in his leg. He howled with pain and slapped her across the face. He pulled her upright by her hair and slapped her again. The Federal Officers in black looked at each other in shock but before they could react Maylin did.

She grabbed Bradley's dangling service revolver and shot him through the chest - without it ever leaving its police issue underarm leather holster.

What stopped the group of young FEDs from opening fire on her, with extreme prejudice, was firstly the fact she'd been brutally assaulted by the large man and secondly that she'd collapsed into unconsciousness on the road as the bullet had left the barrel of the gun.

The projectile ripped through Bradley's chest leaving a rather large exit wound in his back and he collapsed on the floor. The FEDS rushed towards their fallen fellow agent who was now blowing bubbles of blood from his mouth. One of the men tried to stem the flow from the puncture wound.

Seconds later a rumbling started as if an eighteen wheeled juggernaut thundered past. The blue sky seemed to darken, and pieces of concrete started to fall off the overpass. In the distance a bridge collapsed, and a jagged fisher opened up on the hillside looking like the entrance to Hades. Clouds of Californian dirt swirled around the assembled group and one of the FEDS, a local boy, shouted above the cacophony.

"Everyone move; this fucker is off the Richter. Get away from the road!"

The Spaniard picked up Maylin from the hot blacktop and threw her over his shoulder. Overton was grabbed by two of the Feds and helped away from the incident. On mass, they headed away from the highway and up into the San Fernando hills. Just in time too as moments later a large lump of concrete the size of a couch crushed the beautiful 'Cuda's hood and an even larger slab put the dying Agent Bradley out of his misery for good. If they'd have turned back, they'd have seen his feet sticking out from the fallen masonry like a Chuck Jones cartoon. But they didn't and when the earthquake finally stopped all that was left of Bradley and the overhead freeway pass was a mountainous pile of rubble.

Excerpt from the San Fernando Examiner 10th Feb 1971

By Ronald Hernandez

Californians are this morning picking up the pieces of their broken state devastated in the largest earthquake in almost forty years. More than sixty people were killed and thousands injured as a result of yesterday's quake that's inflicted millions of dollars of damage. Moreover, it has left the California's infrastructure, including many new highways, in and around Los Angeles in complete disarray not seen since the Long Beach Earthquake of 1933.

At around 5pm yesterday the fifteen second tremor ripped along a 12-mile fault zone beneath the San Gabriel Mountains at a terrifying magnitude of 6.6. Freeway passes collapsed, hospitals were levelled, power stations outed, and fires caused by burst gas mains erupted across San Fernando and the surrounding area. Thousands of homes, businesses and government agencies have been turned upside down.

Governor Ronald Regan called for calm this morning amongst the general population and praised the work of the police, fire and EMS for tackling the latest disaster to hit the Golden State. He warned people to stay safe and stay away from devastated areas; adding that the national guard were being deployed to aid rescue services but also to ward off potential looters.

In Washing DC President Nixon promised the state as much help as he could muster. He added,

"I have lived in California for many years, and I will do my upmost to ensure that the people of this great country help the people of this great state. The army is being mobilized and we will house those people who have been made homeless by this tragic event. I call on all Californians to stay calm and remember your country and your President are with you."

It is not known if the President's Western White House home ,in San Clemente, has been damaged by this devasting event.

Santa Monica Police Department 2am

He'd been in the interview room for about three hours. He'd fallen sleep within minutes of settling down into the hard upright chair. He could fall asleep anywhere - one of the benefits of being in the military. They tell you to eat, shit or sleep and you make sure you can do it at the drop of a hat. You fail to master that skill, and you get, either kicked out or, in wartime, dead very quickly. He also benefitted from living on the streets of Madrid as a kid and learning to grab a few hours of shut eye when one got the chance

He awoke to the sound of a book being slapped onto the table. Well, it sounded like a book but upon opening his eyes it was a telephone directory. 'OK' he thought is this where they rough me up and leave no bruises. To his surprise a friendly face appeared before his eyes.

"Hola amigo"

It was Jesus, the friendly gypsy cab driver turned senior CIA operative. He smiled wearily at the Spaniard and the Spaniard smiled wearily back.

"I brought you breakfast."

He placed two cups of black coffee on the table and sat down opposite the former British army officer. He offered him a thin black cheroot.

"To early?"

"After the day I've had today not at all!"

Jesus light both the smokes and the men sat in silence for a few minutes savouring the caffeine and the tobacco.

"How's Maylin?"

"She's fine, the doctor's taken a good look at her and given her the all clear. The tranquilizers are mostly out of her system and she's waiting for you in the lobby".

"And Overton?"

"That old hombre is tougher than most men on the force now. The bullet went clean through his wound, they stitched him up and they wanted to keep him in for observation. But he checked himself out and said he needed to get back to his house. Something about feeding the chickens."

Both men smiled. The CIA man stubbed out his cheroot and took a swig from his coffee. He rubbed his eyes; it was way past his bedtime; he figured what with the earthquake and the rogue FBI cell he'd be lucky to get to bed before the end of the decade. He finally looked skyward and laid the whole situation out for the Spaniard.

"OK so here we are. Everything I'm going to tell you is strictly off the record. Nothing is being recorded today; nothing is being transcribed. There are no witnesses just you and me. Dos amigos having a nice little chat."

He took a deep breath

"The federal government will deny any of this took place and if you ever try to reveal what has occurred you will be prosecuted within the upmost severity of the law. Well unless they decide to leave you in a box in the weeds. Do you understand?'

"Yes. No problem."

The Spaniard raised hands in supplication.

"Now you're an ex-cop, a military man and, to be brutally honest, a gun for hire. You understand what I'm saying here."

The Spaniard nodded and Jesus took out an unlabelled manilla folder from his briefcase and laid it onto the table.

"Do you know who Bradley and the Feds were setting you up to assassinate?"

The Spaniard removed a stray piece of tobacco from his mouth.

"Well, I'm guessing not this Dragna guy from the Mob"

"Correct. The man you were about to assassinate was a certain Tomás Borge Martínez cofounder of Sandinista National Liberation Front of Nicaragua. He lives in exile in Columbia and Costa Rica and is very pally with Castro's government in Cuba. He's a communist revolutionary and we, as the American government in no way support any of his activities or that of his colleague Daniel Ortega. He's an intellectual turned guerrilla fighter and commander intent on overthrowing our allies, and by 'our' I mean the current US administration, and by 'allies' I mean the current nationalist government of Nicaragua."

Jesus peered into his paper cup for inspiration and exhaled with exhaustion. He needed more caffeine. He got up and opened the door to the interview room.

"Hey Harry, can we get a couple of cups of coffee in here?"

From far down the corridor a voice replied.

"Sure thing boss."

Within a few seconds two more cups of steaming thick black cop coffee appeared courtesy of a young fresh-faced policeman in crumpled shirt. He promptly placed them onto the desk.

"Anything else sir?"

"No, we're good thanks Harry."

The young man left tucking his shirt into his pants, he'd probably been caught catching forty winks. It went with the job.

"Now where was I?"

Jesus flipped through the file.

"Oh yes our potential victim of the proposed assassination."

Jesus stared directly at him.

"Tomás Borge Martínez is not a friend of the US government, but we haven't, as yet, put him onto any sort of no entry or deportation list. He's in Los Angeles for a conference of political left thinkers, both foreign and domestic, and probably to try and raise some funding for his revolution. We know that he's already being backed by both Cuba and the Soviets."

The Spaniard took a sip of coffee - he wondered what the heck has happened to the Russian he'd encountered in LA. No sign of

Colonel Dmitri or his goons since he'd not taken the shot. I'll keep quiet about that for now, he thought.

"Now the issue here, and I guess the reason you were recruited via Lodestar Operations in London, is because of certain elements or, I should say one element, within the FBI. Let's say it's a leading figure who's trying to restart the ani-communist rhetoric we had here twenty years ago with McCarthy. Politically maybe an admirable notion but realistically way off base. We currently have strong relations with both the Soviet Union and China, and we're bogged down in a war in Vietnam and we, as a government, have no intention of reigniting the Red Menace fear amongst our own population. The government line is detente and negotiation."

Jesus paused and took a sip of coffee he straightened his back and winced. He needed sleep.

"We're trying to control the head of a government agency who practically invented the Agency."

The Spaniard smiled, looked skyward and stretched.

"Is this the Federal one. Are we talking about J. Edgar Hoover?"

Jesus wouldn't even say the name he just nodded,

"The fact that you exist in this whole messy affair is very unfortunate for both the CIA and the Feds."

"Why so?"

Jesus leant into the Spaniard.

"You're a foreign mercenary that was hired by the US government, albeit a covert branch, to kill a foreign politician, unbeknownst to yourself, on US soil. The optics of this are terrible."

The Spaniard picked up the lighter on the table and re-light his cigar. He blew a perfectly formed smoke ring into the air.

"So, what happens now."

"I'll tell you what happens we bury this thing so far into the deepest vaults of the Agency that my grandson's grandson would have trouble finding this disaster. We've already planted a story in the press that the attempt on Martínez's life was by rogue Cuban nationalists from Florida who see any Castro ally as a threat. We'll arrest a few, then quietly release them when this's all died down. Bradley and his dead crew will be put down as killed honourably in the line of duty and the file closed. Those agents still left alive will be reassigned to some far away posting like North Dakota."

He took the said file, closed it and threw it onto the table.

"Which messy business is pretty much wrapped up in a nice little bow - muy bien. There is only one fly left in the in the ointment."

"Me?"

"Yes, you but looking at your record I don't think you're going to be any trouble. Are you?"

Jesus lent forward looking into the Spaniard's eyes. Searching for a deeper understanding; trying to figure out what was going on in his head.

"I'm an over-the-hill mercenary who's broke and looking for an easy life. Gimme the easy option and I'm going to take it."

Jesus smiled and laughed.

"Cabron I've seen you work you're certainly not over the hill but good response and right answer. Look we know you have been paid for your work from Lodestar via a Swiss Bank account. Thomas Fraser, your boss at Lodestar, has told the Brits that much and they kindly passed the information along to us. I don't imagine he'll be recruiting staff for a while."

He continued.

"We're not going to prosecute; we're not even going to kick you out of the country. You're going be given a 90-day tourist, and I mean tourist, visa. Mi Hijo, you get to keep your ill-gotten gains, and you get to have a nice little holiday in California. My guess is that MI6 may want a little chat with you back in London but as you have committed no crimes on British soil or are facing any extradition charges from the US, you are free as a bird."

Jesus tapped the closed file in front of him.

"But considering the nature of what you do and what you're capable of we'd like a little consideration when you're planning any future high jinks. Especially on US soil."

The Spaniard again raised his hands in supplication.

"Hey, I am officially retired as of right now."

"Good, good…"

Jesus pursed his lips, placed his hands together in front of himself and leaned back in his chair. He took another cheroot from the packet on the table and lit it with an old worn zippo lighter. He exhaled blowing grey smoke skyward.

"Now that's agreed there's something else that I wanted to talk to you about."

"You did?"

"Yes, there's odd occasion when people with your unique talents can be very useful to my organisation. Times when we cannot be connected to an event, places we are not allowed to go and countries that it wouldn't be inadvisable for one of our agents to be caught in."

"People like Al, freelancers?"

"Well, we call them contractors."

"Contractors? Does that make it a little more palatable?"

Jesus smiled,

"Yes, I suppose it does. And you'd be a great resource for us as you're fluent in Español. You could do all sorts of good for the Agency south of the boarder. You're ex-military, ex-policia; a perfect fit. You work for us as a contractor and I guarantee we'll get you a good salary, a green card, maybe even a green card for that cute little girlfriend of yours? You can't tell me that the Californian sunshine doesn't agree with you a hell of a lot more than damp old London town."

He smiled at Jesus,

"So now you're trying to recruit me to work in secret for the Agency. Like Bradley did for the Feds?"

"Similar but different. Look think about it. Talk to Al alright?"

Resigned the Spaniard nodded.

"OK I will."

The CIA man had a point he couldn't see himself going back to London; now that his old employer was defunct. He'd been so tight for cash last year he'd almost applied for a job as a security guard at a West London paint factory. Great move from Major in the Royal Marines to night watchman.

"This would be strictly freelance?"

"Well as a contractor you'd be free to choose your work."

"Contractor, I like that…"

"Talk to Al."

"I will."

"You do that Tio."

"Now when do I get the hell out of here?"

2.30am Santa Monica Police Department

The police officer at the reception got him to sign for his personal effects. The Spaniard smiled and took his wrinkled sports jacket, gold Dupont lighter, squashed half a packet of purito cigars and his trusty box wood Taramundi pocketknife. They'd kept the unregistered Walther pistol he'd bought in South Central from the now dead arms dealer. Obviously, they weren't going to let him walk around town with a gun with the serial number filed off. Little did they know that in the thirty odd years since he'd been given the Taramundi knife by his father that it'd probably killed as least as many people as the Walther, if not more!

The desk cop on duty shoved the release forms across the counter. He squinted when signing them; getting old he thought, better get some reading glasses. Thanks god it was only hit short distance that was affected. No one was hiring a marksman who couldn't find his target; it was as much use as impotence in whore house.

He turned around to get his bearings and find the exit to the building. In the corner a florescent ceiling light was blinking on and off, making it difficult to see around the round. Then he saw her, asleep and looking as beautiful as ever, despite the disarray of her hair and the dust covering her clothes. She looked like some sort of Pre-Raphaelite work of art with her tangled hair and the flickering light in the precinct entrance picking up her high cheek bones and her olive skin. With her head resting on her hand and her feet balled up underneath her on the wooden bench she looked stunning. A waif, covered in dirt and exhausted but still stunning.

They exited the glass doors of the cop shop; bedraggled, bloody, covered in dirt and looking for all the world like a pair of refugees from a natural disaster. Which is exactly what they were.

Not a cab in sight and, despite the fact it was supposedly sunny California, a light rain started to descend from the sky making the sidewalk and the road shine and having the opposite effect on their spirits. He took off his crumpled sports jacket and covered Maylin's shoulders and they started to walk down the street and towards the seafront.

Neither one of them spoke, they were too exhausted by the events of the previous 48 hours. Maylin had been checked over by a doctor and debriefed by the Agency; told to keep quiet if she liked her status as a Nicaraguan student studying in America. They'd questioned her extensively about her nationality as a Nicaraguan being the same as that of the hit Tomás Borge Martínez but there was no link between her and the socialist politician. She was purely a bystander caught in the crossfire of deep state government fuck-up. Jesus smiled and held her hands as he debriefed her.

"You've been through a lot. Just move on and forget all about this. Return to your studies and try and put this incident, your roommate's murder and the earthquake behind you."

"And the Spaniard?"

"That's up to you. But as a word of warning, he's a dangerous man to be near."

She smiled and shook her head recognising Jesus's ancestry.

"Señior, you've been away from Central America for too long. He's an emissary from His Holiness compared to most men from my country."

"Si Amiga, you're probably right."

She was jolted put of her thoughts by the honking of a nearby car. The rain was now much heavier, and water splashed onto the sidewalk as a familiar black sedan pulled up curb side and the rear passenger window rolled down. An Eastern European voice hailed them from deep inside the car.

"Spanish, hey Spanish!"

The Spaniard peered into the rear of the car and saw a familiar face. The Russian Embassy's Cultural Attaché Colonel Dmitry.

"Come on Spanish get in, get in…"

The now soaking wet mercenary waved the car away.

"Last time I did that I ended up being tortured by your goons."

The car jerkily drove along the street as the driver tried to keep pace with the two pedestrians. Stop, go, stop go.

"Look Spanish I'm, sorry let me give you a ride. We need to talk; I promise not the funny business."

He stopped in the pouring rain and looked across at Maylin who shrugged,

"It beats this weather" she commented.

They both got into the car; it was warm and dry. Dmitry sat in the corner of the rear seats allowing both plenty of space. It was a relief to be out of the rain. Despite the disagreeable company, it was a far better atmosphere than what was on offer outside.

Dmitry signalled for the car's driver to go. The man turned round and nodded. He smiled at the Spaniard who recognised the face. It was the same man who smiled at him from across the street from the botched hit. The same blonde-haired Russian who'd trained a sniper rifle, probably a Dragunov, on him. Had he assassinated Martinez the Spaniard knew this man would have put a bullet in him.

"There, there how much better it is to be out of the rain."

Like a father concerned for his two children Dmitry handed them a blanket to soak up some of the rainwater.

"Please, please."

He then, as if from nowhere magicked up two steel cups with a shot of vodka in each.

"For your health."

"And yours."

The Spaniard and Maylin both gulped down the clear white spirit. The alcohol burning their throats but providing them with kick of warmth to drive out the cold. He did ponder for a moment whether the Soviets could be trying to poison them. They do have a history of getting rid of enemies of the state in this fashion but by now he was too exhausted to care and figured the risk was minimal. Plus, he could now see the

Russian was also enjoying a cup of his nation's famed spirit.

"So, you are thinking why is the Russian Cultural Attaché picking us up in his very nice American imperialist vehicle?"

"It did cross my mind."

"Maybe you think that we mean you and the lady harm?"

"Well, you did tie me to a chair in a deserted warehouse and torture me."

"Such strong words. We question, merely question!"

Dmitry took the bottle of Stolichnaya balanced between his knees and poured them both another shot of vodka. He continued,

"You see I want to make sure you understand that we are friends and that the Soviet Union wants not to pursue any vengeance against either yourself or your friends, such as the very beautiful *zhenschina* here".

He helped himself to a shot of the vodka, straight from the bottle.

"Our role here was to stop the Americans killing one of our allies in Nicaragua. We do not wish to take over the country, but we wish it to be free to choose its own destiny. It is purely the same goal as your bosses in the West have. We do not want trouble, we do not want war, now is a time for as the French say détente. This FBI man Hoover is like our Russian father Stalin, a strong leader but now out of his time. The future is better if we all can try to get along. Like squabbling siblings, we will always fight over the toys, but we are fellow citizens of this world are we not?"

He was smiling at both like a benevolent father. The car rumbled along Pacific Avenue splashing puddles onto the sidewalk, devoid of people at this late hour. Despite this the lights from hotels, bars and shops remained on. They illuminated a rain-soaked Santa Monica creating an almost magical and ethereal scene. It was as if the rain was washing away the trauma of the past leaving merely a rose-tinted memory. The vodka helped.

The Spaniard stared straight ahead; one thousand yards. He was thinking back over the past few days. Coming to America, meeting Maylin, the murder of her friend, her kidnapping and the aborted assassination. It brought up all sorts of memories, from the death of his wife in Malaya to the myriad of warzones and conflicts he'd fought in for more than twenty years. The faces of those he'd killed, of which many were burned onto his memory for life. The nightmares he had from his days as a child in Asturias and Madrid to the horrors of the war in SE Asia; the heat and the thick steaming Malay jungle that he'd fought in. He so desperately wanted to be free from those memories. He took a swig of the Russian vodka but knew that wouldn't even touch the sides of those mental images.

The car came to a standstill.

"Your hotel Spanish? Or can we take you back to the lady's house."

"No Colonel this will do fine."

"Before you go Spanish, I have a present."

"You're not going to try and recruit me, are you?"

Dmitry looked puzzled and then smiled.

"No, my friend we only recruit those who believe in our Marxist-Leninist ideology. You've spent too many years fighting against our side. We know of your true loyalties. As degenerate and capitalistic as they are."

The Spaniard thought of the irony of such a statement from a man wearing a bespoke silk suit and being chauffeur driven in a very expensive automobile. But as the Colonel may have said himself 'the spoils they go to victor.'

The Colonel motioned to the tall blonde Russian in the front passenger seat who passed him a box.

"This is for you just a little present from the people of the Soviet Union for you not to forget us when you choose your next operation. Maybe you choose not to upset either us or our friends."

The Spaniard opened it to see twenty-five Cohiba Esplendidos long and thick Churchill sized cigars in a wonderful cedar wood box. These were usually the preserve of El Presidente, Castro himself, and usually reserved for very special heads of state or diplomats. He'd heard of them, but he'd never smoked one and he opened it up inhaling deeply.

"Well Colonel I shall take these in the spirit that they are intended, and I will think fondly of you every time I smoke one. Thank you."

"I prefer you think more fondly of my people and my country. Then maybe, just maybe we'll meet again in happier times. And remember … Staryy drug luchshe dvukh novykh."

"What does it mean?"

"An old friend is better than two new ones."

The Ocean Hotel - Santa Monica

They had nowhere else to go, Maylin's bungalow in Venice would still be playing host to forensics from Santa Monica PD. All exits and entrances would be sealed off for a while yet with sawhorses, police tape and possibly the odd patrolman. It was the hotel or the sidewalk.

Even thought it was after 3am the streets of Santa Monica were still alive with party goers and the people of the night. Some were starting work, some finishing and some just out for a good time; that at this hour was probably going to turn bad. The streets were full of the revellers' detritus, beer bottles, cigarette stubs and paper, strewn all around. Even the beach wasn't free from the odd newspaper or hotdog wrapper. But as the lights from the pier and the glow from the moon hit the waves of the bay it seemed to make up for all the man-made trash. Romantic decay described the scene perfectly as the entered the hotel and made their way up to the room.

They entered holding other's hands in complete darkness. As the Spaniard went to switch on the main light by the door, they heard a click from the corner. There was nothing to see apart from a small red glowing dot. Suddenly the lamp by the window was switched on revealing a large man sitting in an old brown hotel chair smoking a cigarette. In his other hand was a small black pistol pointed squarely at them both, deadly at this range.

"Santa Mierda!"

Shouted Maylin as she recoiled from the man.

"Hello, love birds I'm here on behalf of London."

It was Collins the man who'd been sent by Fraser at Lodestar to 'clean up' this situation stateside and make sure it couldn't be linked to London.

The Spaniard stepped forward angry as hell. Not caring that there was a gun pointed straight at his chest.

"Jesus Christ, who the fuck are you and what do you want?"

"Calm down Pancho Villa, before you or the lady get hurt."

The man extinguished his cigarette and leaned forward.

"Lodestar sent me to clean up the mess here but I'm a bit bloody confused about what I'm supposed to be cleaning up. It looks like you've done half of my job for me, killing that FBI yank. Which leaves me with only a couple of loose ends … you two."

The Spaniard stepped forward and quizzically regarded the hulking man.

"Hang on a minute, I know you. You're Collins that Sergeant Major from Oman, I worked with you."

"Yes, Oman I've been there. Now shup up fella and let me talk."

"No, I won't, if you're working for Fraser in London why don't you call him and see what he has to say?"

"Fuck off, you're trying to buy time, time you don't have!"

"Call London!"

The Spaniard stepped forward menacingly, despite the threat of the gun.

"If I'm wrong you can shoot us both." The Spaniard pointed towards the phone.

Collins kept the pistol on them and looked them over to gauge reactions. The black telephone was next to the bed. He would have to get up to use it. He gestured towards it with his gun.

"You do it amigo."

Maylin backed slightly out of the way and the Spaniard picked up the phone, asked the front desk for an outside line and got the operator to put a call through to a number in Whitehall, London. The phone rang and rang, and he offered the receiver to Collins. Collins nodded and, without ever lowering his pistol, he took the handset. It was answered on the fourth ring.

"Hello."

Collins cleared his throat; he didn't recognise the male voice on the other end.

"'ello who's this? Can I speak to Fraser?"

"Mr Fraser isn't here. I'm Detective Sergeant Stevens with the Metropolitan police now how can I help…"

Before the cop on the other side of the pond could finish his sentence Collins gently cradled the phone with a small ding and sat back into his chair. He smiled, still training his gun on them both.

"Ahh, it would appear that I am now unemployed and I ain't gonna get paid for this assignment."

He stood up out of the chair and ran a hand through his silver hair.

"Now the question is what to do with you two?'

The Spaniard smiled,

"Well, I could give you two thousand reasons you should just leave. How does that sound?",

Collins smiled back at him.

"I really should shoot both of you it'll be the final connection between you and London and me. Plus, you've seen me face now, haven't you?"

"Collins, I saw your face back in Oman"

"That's true. Awww bugger,"

Collins looked the man hard in the eye and rubbed a large callused had against his chin. He paused looking skyward for inspiration. There was a careful balancing act going on here in the mind of this toughened soldier of fortune. Should he just shoot these two and disappear, maybe have a long weekend in Las Vegas and then back to Blighty. Alternatively, he could take the cash and disappear like a ghost, no come back, no repercussions and no guilt. The man was a Spic, but he was also a former British officer for Christ's sake; you don't shoot your own or at least you try to avoid it.

"I don't know what to do. How much cash have you got?"

"Just over two thousand dollars in per diems and it's all yours."

"I must be getting fuckin' soft."

Collins slowly lowered his pistol and put the weapon back inside his jacket. He stubbed out his cigarette and straightened his tie.

"That sounds fine Sir."

The Spaniard went to the bedside cabinet and handed over a small buff envelope of cash to the British mercenary. Collins checked the amount and pocketed it. He smiled, it which was pretty good seeing as no one got killed.

"Thank you, Sir."

Collins had now adopted the role of NCO towards a senior ranking officer, as the Spaniard was now affectively his new employer. He moved towards the door reaching for the handle. He suddenly spun round to face them both.

"By the way if you ever need some muscle for a job, I'm still available for hire. I believe Lodestar are out of business so if you hear of any 'eavy lifting that's required please get in touch Sir. After all, us old soldiers have got to stick together, haven't we Major?"

The Spaniard smiled.

"Yes, Sergeant you're right."

He didn't know why he asked the next question, but he did, probably just common courtesy,

"And how are we supposed to get hold of you? Sergeant?"

"My card Sir."

Collins handed him a white business card which just had Collins' name, a telephone number and, what he supposed was his company name, Executive Orders.

"My number's on my card Sir"

"In the Middle East?"

"Nah East London. It's me mum's council flat in Bermondsey. She'll know how to get hold of us. I'll be off then."

The gun for hire turned to leave but paused half-way through the door.

"Would you recommend swimming in the Pacific Ocean?"

Maylin and the Spaniard both nodded in astonishment at the question.

"I must try that then, it looks inviting."

And with that the menacing form of the former Regimental Sergeant Major left. He was gone as quickly as he appeared out of the darkness just leaving a waft of American cigarettes and a hint of gun oil. They locked then bolted the door, placing a chair underneath the handle, and collapsed together onto the bed. They were asleep in seconds.

One month later - Venice Beach - Late Spring

After the earthquake he'd gone down to Pacific Coast Highway to find the station wagon, but it'd been towed by the local law. He picked it up in a pound just outside of Santa Monica. He figured he owed it to the owner, Josephia's boyfriend, the now deceased roommate of Maylin. The woman's body had been flown back to her family in Nicaragua, the perpetrators of the murder were both dead, but the case was still active.

The car as well seemed to be still functioning, all it took was a can of gasoline and it was up and running; albeit still leaking fuel via the bullet holes. When the boyfriend finally returned his call, he seemed reluctant to pick up the car and it sat for a few weeks behind Maylin's bungalow in Venice. The Spaniard eventually offered the man a couple to hundred dollars to take it off his hands and he willingly accepted. Maybe he didn't want to be reminded of his dead girlfriend or maybe he just didn't want the car.

Either way the Spaniard ended up with it. He intended to eventually give it to Maylin as local transport, but it needed to be refurbished first. So, as the Spring turned toward the Summer, he decided to use part of his 90-day-tourist-visa to fix the fourteen-year-old Nash Rambler wagon. It wasn't that it was in that bad state of repair it just needed a little love and tenderness. After cleaning the whole thing out, he set about putting four new tyres onto the thing for a start. He went back to the gas station on PCH and bought some nice new rubber off the young man who'd given him the directions to Overton's house.

"Hey you're back."

The blonde Californian kid was wiping oil off his hands with a rag from his back pocket when the Spaniard pulled up.

"You want me to get those tires for you mister?"

"Yes, I do and I may have a little work for you as well."

"Well, I rarely turn down the opportunity to make some money."

It turned out the kid, Jim, was an engineering major at UCLA and his parents owned the gas station. The Spaniard made him an offer to come and help him fix the car and he was more than happy to help. Overton also lent a hand helping to fit a new fuel tank, service the engine and get the old girl back on the road. By the time they fixed the Rambler it ran like a dream despite the fact there was not a single panel that wasn't missing paint, rusted or dented. It was no work of art but was a very reliable means of transport. Dented on the outside but running smooth on the interior - sounded like the Spaniard himself.

So, by night he lived and loved Maylin in the tiny wooden cottage near Vencie Beach. By day, as she went back to her studies at UCLA or to work at the record store, he worked out own demons on this old car with a young man and a very old one. Six weeks of hard work later they were finished.

One morning he was sat drinking coffee on the tailgate of the station wagon. He watched the rolling mist across the bay slowly clear to reveal what he thought would be a glorious Californian day. This is what they called the beginnings of May Gray - when the weather was changeable in So-Cal before the summer really kicks in. His attention as brought back to reality with the honk of a car horn. Sitting in a silver shark of a car across the road was a black man in a black straw trilby hat and a grey silk shirt.

"Hey Limey, wanna grab breakfast?"

It was Al smiling and beckoning him over.

"OK but you're buying."

"The story of my life!"

Diner, Santa Monica Beach, Morning

They were sat in a train car diner overlooking the bay. The same red vinyl and silver aluminium diner as before. They were their usual booth, back to the wall and good visuals on the front door and the rear. You could take the military men out of the field, but you can't take the field out of the man.

The waitress poured them each coffee, the Spaniard had it black, and Al took it with cream and sugar. She left them with the menus to choose their food and the two men sat for a moment in silence. Al took out a packet of cigarettes and light up. Exhaling smoke he smiled and looked at the Spaniard.

"Enjoying your ninety-day visa?"

"It's good. I've been fixing up that old station wagon. Then maybe a trip across the border into Mexico. Who knows? Hey, has there been any more reaction to that rogue FBI cell that Bradley was running?"

"Nah they've gone very quiet about that. It's been quashed from the top."

"The top? How far did it go?"

"All the way man, all the way."

Within a year of the foiled assassination of the Nicaraguan dissident Martinez, J Edgar Hoover, was dead from a heart attack so ending his almost forty-year career as head of the FBI, having swerved under six Presidents. He was implicated in various sandals involving illegal wiretapping, burglary, bribery and blackmail. Most of it was never proven as Hoover's long-term secretary Helen Gandy was already destroying any incriminating files as the two men drank their coffee in Santa Monica eleven months before the death of the FBI boss.

Al lit another cigarette,

"Have you given any thought to what Jesus proposed to you. Working as a contractor for the Agency?"

"Not really. Let me guess you've got a job offer?"

"Whoa slow-down amigo, nothing firm I'm here to test the water."

"I see, test the water?"

The waitress returned and they both ordered. Al had eggs over easy with bacon and pancakes and for the Spaniard just an order of French toast. She departed towards the kitchen.

"What's the job?"

"So, you are interested? Getting bored playing pattycake with el Señorita?"

"It's 'La' not 'El' in Spanish. And no, I could never get bored of that Al!"

"I can imagine."

Both men laughed, smoked and drank coffee. Then silence. Al pipped up out of nowhere,

"It's nothing major. A surveillance job down in Florida. We're being asked to keep an eye on some Cuban nationalists who want to overthrow Castro … again. They're a breakaway branch of the Movimiento Nacionalista Cubano or MNC. It's the usual thing; they lobby congress for more sanctions against Cuba, they're linked to a bomb threat on the Cuban UN ambassador, they have a small training camp outside Tampa and their dream is another Bay of Pigs. Exactly what Uncle Sam doesn't want. The agency has got them under surveillance and wire tapped. They want a couple of outside guys just to monitor their activities, take notes and report back. Nothing too heavy."

"Sounds like a baby siting job anyone could do."

"Exactly and that's why I thought of you.

They both smiled and Al continued.

"No seriously it'd be a help to have someone backing me up who hable's the Espanol."

"Maybe, I don't know. Look I'm thinking of taking off down south. I've never been to Latin America and I thought it'd be fun to visit a Spanish speaking country, since I haven't been to one in around twenty years."

Al leaned back and sized up the man.

"Look, it's an easy gig one hundred and fifty a day plus expenses and maybe six weeks work. Think about it. Plus, it'd probably help me to get you a green card so you could stay stateside. You can take that holiday whenever."

"I'll think about it."

"You do that. You still got that Nixon pardon?"

"I have. You never know when you're gonna need the help of El Presidente."

"Ain't that the truth."

Their food came and both men began to eat the breakfast of champions, the American version of that meal anyway.

July 1971 - Santa Monica - Sunset

They'd packed their car that morning, trying to work out what they needed for the three-thousand-mile journey. They'd be travelling through Mexico, Guatemala and El Salvador before they made it to Nicaragua. A couple of suitcases full of clothes, magazines, books and some basic bedding; just in case they had to use the car as overnight accommodation. The map was on the dash and the petrol tank was full. and were ready to hit the road. Pacific Coast Highway: a gateway to the Mexican border to the south was calling them. Tonight, though belonged to them.

They said their farewells in style at the restaurant they'd had their first date in. Maylin's fellow students from UCLA, a friend from the record store, mechanic Jim, Overton and even Al had joined them at La Casa Carlos in Santa Monica and enjoyed some great Mexican fayre. All of them full on burritos, quesadillas and far too many cervezas they'd enjoyed the company until the wee small hours.

Al ordered a fresh round of beers and Margaritas. He spoke to the assembled group.

"I can't believe you two are driving all the way to Managua."

Overton laughed,

"I can't believe you think that bucket of rust is gonna make it all the way to Nicaragua!".

The Spaniard responded to the heckler,

"Says the man with the oldest Studebaker in California"

"She's vintage - just like me - still going strong after all these years."

Jim jumped to the defence of his mechanics,

"She looks like hell but that Rambler's good for a few thousand miles yet. Plus no one South of the border is gonna want to steal her, she looks like a beat-up pussycat, but she's got the heart of a lion. I know I did most of the work."

"You've got the hands of a surgeon Jim."

The Spaniard raised a glass of red towards the young blonde Californian boy who smiled and raised a bottle of beer back at him.

As the night came to an end the friends all bid each other adios and slowly disappeared into the night. Al hugged Maylin and shook hands with the Spaniard.

"You kids have fun down south but not too much fun, if you get my drift."

He went to get up and dropped his car keys. As he went to pick them up his hat fell off. He began to laugh. The Spaniard slapped him on the back.

"You're too far gone to drive amigo. You're staying with us tonight."

Al picked up his straw hat, sat back down and lit a cigarette.

"Ok, ok no argument from me."

The work the two men had completed in Florida had, as promised, been mundane but very lucrative. Just over eight weeks of sitting in a car and taking photographs of a training camp, listening in to illegal wire taps and monitoring the comings and goings of the group. Sometimes they were outside of Tampa in the swamplands watching teenage boys trying to hit targets on a Cuban owned ranch with old World War Two M1 rifles. On other occasions they were monitoring the group at rallies on the streets of Ybor City.

Once the Spaniard had gone to a church hall in Ybor as a spectator to watch the group's leaders try and raise funds from the Cuban exiles in a bid to take back the motherland. He sat between an old Cuban mestizo grandmother and a middle-aged cigar store owner. After all the speeches both of whom seemed to think that despite their hatred for Castro they didn't want to go back to the motherland. Ignacio, the store owner, said to him

"I like the idea of taking back Havana, but I want to stay here in Ybor! My kids were born here and to be honest they got a better future in Florida than back in Cuba."

Notes were taken, phone calls recorded and pictures of poorly trained men in fatigues and older men in straw hats were captured. All of which was stuffed into a folder and sent to a government contact in Langley. Where they'd, more than likely, sit in a filing cabinet for the next twenty years before being archived or destroyed. The work was boring, mundane but lucrative and had given him a green card. So, the wet dark streets of London were no longer all he had to look forward to. He had enough money to live on for the next few years and if he picked up the occasional contract job with Al, all the better.

He mused these thoughts as he started to drift off to sleep next to Maylin. For the first time in a long time, he felt hopeful about the future and what lay ahead for them. He thought he heard the sound of a bell, maybe a boat out on the bay, but it could have just been his imagination. Then sleep and for the first time in many years no dreams of death, destruction or the horrors of war.

July 1971 - Santa Monica - Sunrise

A purple, then orange, then yellow and finally bright white glow appeared rising out of the desert to the east. The Spaniard bid a fond farewell to Al who'd strolled off to get breakfast and then retrieve his car from the Mexican restaurant's parking lot. The black man shook his hand and clasped his back. A move that the Spaniard found endearing, very un-British but very Spanish; a culture he left decades ago and one he was hoping to rediscover as he headed south.

"Good luck man and stay outta trouble. But if you need help remember we got contacts down there all the way from Tijuana to Costa Rica."

"Thanks Al. I promise this is going to be purely a vacation. No busman's holiday for me."

Al looked confused.

"Is that a Limey thing?"

"It's a Limey thing."

The two men shook hands, and the Spaniard opened the car door allowing Al to get inside his large silver shark of a Chevy Impala.

"Goodbye my friend."

"Let's call it hasta luego."

"Hasta luego it is."

And with that the ex-County Sheriff's cop drove off in a cloud of dust, the car's V8 rumble was still audible even though the car disappeared over the brow of a hill. The Spaniard walked back to the small bungalow, he could see Maylin outside witing to get into the car. She was dressed in a faded pair of jeans, an old t-shirt and sandals but she still managed to look like she'd stepped off a catwalk; to him anyway.

Maylin had finished college and was not due back until the Fall. They had three months to cover more than six thousand miles there and back and if the Rambler didn't make it, he figured they could always buy another car or just hop on a big silver bird; it was 1971 after all.

The smiled at each other as they got into the car. He was driving and she was in charge of navigation. As he started the car he looked across at Maylin and smiled she leaned over and kissed him passionately.

"I want you to see the real Nicaragua and the real me with my family."

"Sounds good to me."

He put his arm around her and put the car into D for drive and they pulled out into the road heading for the 405. They were bound for San Diego, and he felt for the first time, in a long time, that things were heading in the right direction. He mused that he must really tell her the whole of his life story and how since he left his home in Asturias, he'd been nothing more than a stranger in numerous strange lands.

As the car picked up speed in the warm California sunshine, and the ocean came into view from the west, he also thought - I really should tell her my real name.

The End

DISCLAIMER

This is a work of fiction, the names, characters, places, businesses, events and incidents are either the products of this author's fevered imagination or used in a fictitious manner. Any resemblance to actual persons, living or dead, or actual events is purely coincidental.

Anyway, like I've got the time to properly research each individual character from real life and steal their actual lives. Sorry I'm too busy; that would take an age!

That being said, there are a few people in this book who exist or actually existed. J Edgar Hoover for one, and to be honest I've only referenced him in passing and said nothing about his supposed homosexuality or his cross-dressing but there I've said it. I know you were thinking about that, I was, and I smiled when I did. The other characters in this book who share the same names as people in real life include Paul Dragna; the son of West Coast crime boss Jack Dragna. This is purely coincidental and the Dragna family as far as I am concerned have no blemish on their reputation or character. I have no desire to wind up in a box in the weeds.

The other person who I have mentioned in this work of fiction is Tomás Borge Martínez. He was a cofounder of the Sandinista National Liberation Front in Nicaragua and was Interior Minister of Nicaragua during one of the administrations of Daniel Ortega. He was also a renowned statesman, writer, and politician. I have no knowledge of his visit to Los Angeles in 1971 or any other year and I have no idea if there was an attempted assassination on American soil. I think not, but hey I cannot confirm this. Again, I have used his name as a symbol of all revolutionary figures from South and Central America during this time. He represents an amalgamation of more than a dozen characters.

One of the other aspects of this book is the inclusion of the 1971 San Fernando Earthquake. I have used this (and I apologise in advance, but I am an old hack) as a Deux Ex Machina: a god-like plot device to tie up all the loose ends. I had been reading all about the event near Sylmar and it was one of the events I really wanted to include in my book. Unfortunately for all you historians out there I have the correct day of the event that of Tuesday 9th February 1971 but the wrong time. This event took place at 6am whereas I have, for literary purposes placed it at 5pm. I apologise but let's not forget this is a work of fiction from my restless mind!

Finally, I have mentioned a place and a person from the SE Asian island of Penang in Malaysia. Firstly, the place is the Bellevue Hotel; a beautiful building set in the jungle that sits a-top Penang Hill overlooking the Indian Ocean. It is an actual place, and I thoroughly encourage anyone to pay them a visit. The former owner was a Mr William Halliburton - a Sheriff of the island when it was still part of the British Empire. He is of no relation to the Mr Halliburton who runs the hotel when our main protagonist and his wife stay there. I just liked the name. Although beware if you do visit the hotel there are green vipers who slither through the vines above the veranda. As the sign there says 'Leave them alone and they will leave you alone'.

Richard J. Green November 1st 2024.

Printed in Great Britain
by Amazon